GHOST DAYS

ASHER ELBEIN
TIFFANY TURRILL

ISBN: 978-1-7329764-0-5
]
Library of Congress Control Number: 2018966599

Front cover image and internal illustrations by Tiffany Turrill
Book design copyright Emily Horne

Printed by PrintNinja
Printed in China

First Printing, January 2019

Campanian Press
1009 East 13 Street
Austin, Texas, 78702

asherelbein.com
tiffanyturrill.com

To my family and friends,
who accompanied me to higher mountains.

TABLE OF CONTENTS

I'm just a poor wayfaring stranger
Traveling through this world of woe
There is no sickness, no toil nor danger
In that bright land to which I go.

—"Wayfaring Stranger," American folk song

"All we want here is to get the most we can out of this country, as quick as we can, and get out."
—Northern lumber manager quoted in *Our Southern Highlanders*, Horace Kephart, 1913

THE WAMPUS MASK

1900

The day before she made the trade, Anna O'Brien woke to an empty cabin and an empty bed. She'd surfaced hard from strange dreams of black lakes, deep under the stone, surfaced and reached out to find him gone with only rumpled, clammy bedding in his place. A fading whisper of warmth on the mattress. Nothing more.

It wasn't the first time she'd risen to find herself alone. In the year since they'd been married, Tom had often left before sunrise, sliding out carefully so as not to wake her. She'd do the things that needed doing, any of a hundred tasks to keep the homeplace running; grind cornmeal, mend clothing, haul water up from the cold creek when the rain didn't come. Tom would return by late afternoon, loping down out of the trees in his broad-brimmed hat, with a brace of rabbits or a possum in his hand. Sometimes he came back the next day, and sometimes he came back with nothing. He always came back.

But that morning Anna felt a strange disquiet. A faint glow crept through the cracks in the shutters, the trees whispering outside. Cool air prickled on her skin. She lay a while, a rawboned, dark-haired girl staring at the threadbare pillow, brow furrowed as she tried to work out what was wrong. There was nothing she could put her finger on; nothing definite. Just her heart beating sluggishly in her chest. Just the rustling of distant leaves, the morning hush, and the empty bed.

Anna blew a wisp of hair out of her face. Hauling herself up, she slipped on a gingham dress and opened the shutters, soft light flowing in over the hanging quilt and table, the stone chimney, the log walls packed with mud and grass to keep out the weather. Stripping the mattress, she shook out the linens and the wedding quilt, folding them up with the washing. She was just scraping a bit of preserve on some cold cornbread when she heard the crunch of footsteps on the path.

"Morning!"

"Morning," Anna called, opening the door. Milly's tired face peered up at her from the edge of the narrow plot, her blond hair tousled by the walk, a small burlap sack under her arm. "Come in!"

The other woman came up to the porch, brushing the twigs off her dress before she swept inside. "Where's Tom at?"

"Hunting."

"Well, I just come up to bring y'all that flour. And I wanted to see if you got any meat left over you can spare? John ain't shot a thing in two weeks and he's getting stormy about it, right stormy, so I thought I might cook him something special."

Anna went up on tiptoes to look at the top of the cupboard, pulling out a jar of cured meat. "We still got a bit of that bear Tom shot a while back—"

"That'd be nice," Milly said.

Anna passed it over. She bobbed on her feet a moment, unsure. "You… got Clarabelle minding the baby? Time to sit a spell?"

Milly shot her a surprised look, but she set the flour sack down on the wooden tabletop by the cupboard, pulled out a stool and sat, crossing her legs under her plaid dress. "Just a spell, thank you. I guess you heard about Virgil?"

Anna hadn't. A welter of O'Briens lived down the little valley and along the neighboring branches, all of them Tom's people, all of them woven together in a wall of talk and gossip and past experience she had no idea how to climb. Nor had many been inclined to come up to the top of the holler, where their home squeezed up on the last narrow strip of good land, and the chestnuts and ash trees closed in beyond. Milly O'Brien was the only one to look in every now and then, and Anna was always quietly pleased to see her. She filled the cabin up.

They sat a while, nibbling on cornbread, Milly catching her up on the news. Virgil —Tom's second cousin, didn't she recall him?— had cursed the stone soil and walked off his plot, taking his family and going down to distant Madisonville to cut trees, part of a steady trickle of people leaving the neighboring valleys. Sara O'Brien was in a family way again, her fourth. A holy roller had come into the holler to preach God and damn fiddle music, damn the play parties for leading young people into dancing, and wasn't that just nonsense? Somewhere down in the foothills, companies bought up big tracts, put people living there on the lease or ran them out. Hard times coming for some.

"Think it'll come up here?" Anna said.

"Don't reckon it will," Milly said, waving a hand. "High up the mountain as we are. Where's Tom find such hunting anyhow? He's got some luck, that man."

Anna ducked her head, smiling. "Up the cliffs? Says there's still good game up that way."

"Nora better not hear that. John said he might head up that way and she looked like she was fixing to tell him to go cut her a switch."

"Can you imagine?"

"He'd do it, too," Milly said. She rose and stretched, tucking the jar under her arm. "I'd best be on my way. Thanks for the meat, and John thanks you right well, too. Or he will."

"Milly—" Anna opened the door for her and paused. "You ever… get a bad feeling when John goes out?"

"Oh, he takes his rifle and bag down and I just worry sick," Milly said. "But then, I always do. So I guess I'm used to it by now. Take care, dear."

She sat on the porch a while after Milly left, staring out into the ash and chestnut trees, listening to the birds flitting among the heavy boughs. Ridgelines swept out beyond the narrow valley, green quilts shifting under the turning clouds. Smears of rain drifted on the horizon. On the mountainside, sandstone cliffs loomed grey and crumbling above the summer canopies. Tom was up there now, more likely than not, stealing along the base of the rocks, stopping to examine sign, or to pocket soft lead bullets left over from bushwackers during the war. There were plenty of those, he told her once, and other things too: arrowheads and markings deep in the rock crevasses, and sometimes bones thrown down in the gullies, surrounded by faded blue cloth…

Milly might worry, but Anna seldom did. There was too much to be done, a wedded rhythm of hard work, and Tom at the center of it. She loved him with a desperate hunger, the steadiness of him, the crookedness of his expression, the flowers and bullets he brought her from the trees. The scratch of his beard on her cheek. If she was sometimes lonely, if their food often ran low, if she often clung tightly to him at night, feeling the bellows-working of his breath — that was life. She missed him sometimes, when he was out in the forest. But she did not worry about him.

And yet.

Anna shook her head. Standing, she fetched the broom and swept the cabin floor, losing herself in the motion of the bristles, working back and forth over the floorboards, sweeping it as clean as it had ever been. When she finished, she looked out the open door at the trees and then swept again.

Noon tilted into afternoon. Leaves rattled and spun in the yellow light. Anna took a bucket up to the seep above the little corn field, balancing on fallen logs as she went. Spongy wood and moss crumbled under her feet. When she returned, she set the bucket down on the porch and tried to do the washing. But the smell of him was all over it, a musky note against the woodsmoke and sweet goldenrod on the breeze, and for a moment she was lost, staring out into the woods.

"Being a fool," she said to herself. "He's fine. He'll be back soon enough."

So she scrubbed at the linens and clothing for a while, carried them back and hung them up on the line behind the cabin. Then she went back inside and set about baking a few loaves of bread, kneading her frustration out in the dough before putting it aside to let it rise.

But it did not rise. The sun dropped toward the rocky cliffs, and the blue-green gloom filtered through the tree trunks. Anna began to pace in circles around the cabin, going out onto the porch to look out into the darkening forest, her dress rustling against her legs. The birds outside had been quiet, strangely so. Once or twice she thought she heard distant gunshots, carried down the mountainside by the wind. But they were faint, and gone before she could be sure.

She lit a pair of lanterns and hung them in the windows, before going out to the woodpile and pulling out a pair of small logs.The ghostly shapes of the washing shuddered on the line as she closed the door. She built a little fire in the stone hearth and sat back on the bed, blowing out a heavy breath, her foot tapping, staring at the window at the dusk. Something oppressive and tight spread itself in the space behind her eyes.

Something howled, desperate and miserable in the dark. All at once the nervous energy coiling inside Anna exploded outward and she darted toward the door, her hand closing over a kitchen knife as she went. Snatching a lantern, she tore the door open. Tree trunks and twigs shone in the flickering light, the rasping calls of tree frogs echoing through the gloom.

Brush crackled in the forest. Anna's knuckles strained on the lantern handle. What was she doing? She should go inside, now, lock the door and sit by the fire, let whatever it was pass. But her legs were locked in place, there on the threshold. She squinted out into the dark, the crack of branches growing louder, louder—

It exploded out of the woods, pale and staring, its mouth stretched wide, arms tearing at its own flesh. Anna yelped in surprise and jumped back, holding up the knife, in time to see it trip over the side of the porch and fall heavily against the boards. It lay there, shivering and twitching, and looked up at her with wide eyes that rolled in their sockets like those of a panicked horse. Eyes she knew.

"Tom?" she whispered.

Her husband jerked at the sound of her voice. Blood streamed from the cuts in his arms and chest, black in the shaking lantern light. His clothing was in tatters, his prized hat missing, the hunting jacket ripped to shreds. His mouth worked soundlessly, and as Anna stared down at him she realized he was trying, and failing, to scream.

***

They gathered in the cabin, kith and kin crowding into the small room and clustering out on the porch, faces drawn and pale. Weak sunlight played on rough homespun cloth, on dresses and open shirts. Milly gnawed a knuckle by the chimney. On the bed, something shook beneath the quilt.

Anna sat on the floor beside the mattress, her knees drawn up. The murmur washed over her like wind on the treetops. She'd lost track of how long it had taken to coax Tom into the bed, to calm his violent shaking, to get him to drink, the water in the ladle spilling over his tattered shirt. She'd curled up beside him, helpless, holding his quaking body through a night that never seemed to end; only when the sun crested the top of the mountain and touched the cabin did he give a ragged sigh and fall asleep. That was when she'd rushed down the path to hammer on doors, crying out for help. Younger family members running the word down the holler, a growing crowd gathering up at the cabin. Old Nora O'Brien coming up last, hobbling up the path, her face grim.

Now Nora laid a heavy, wrinkled hand against Tom's forehead. "Well, he ain't shook himself out, yet. That's something."

"Is he sick?" Anna's voice shook.

Carpen' Jim ran nervous fingers through his beard, dislodging bits of sawdust. "Looks scratched up, powerful scratched. Might be a catamount lit on him? Put him in a bad way?"

Nora's mouth tightened. She was a stooped woman, but stooped like a tree root, curving and iron-hard. "Look at his eyes. Something's scared him right bad. Scared the ghost out of him. There's worse in the woods 'n catamounts. Worse up 'n the cliffs. Tom, you fool boy. You knowed better. I taught you better." Her hand quivered a little on his forehead and she drew it away. "Had to show off for your pretty new wife. And now he's haint-touched. Haint-touched, or yee-wahed—"

Tom shifted in bed. "*Ewah...*"

Anna was at his side in a heartbeat. "Tom? Tom, it's me. It's me—"

"*Ewah.*" The word slurred out, toneless from cracked lips. His eyes twitched. "*E… wah.*"

"He's seen the devil or somelike," one of the old men rumbled. "Lost his wits. I seen it come back in the war. Men cracking under the gun-thunder. Walking like the dead. Some come back, but I never knowed a one so broke inside to get right."

"He ain't been under the guns. Witched, maybe?"

"We ain't never had witch trouble here."

"Can we—" Anna said. "Can we send for—"

Nora crossed her arms over her patched apron. "No use. He's far gone, Anna. Far gone. No preacher'll help him. No medicine we got, either. If he were witched—if he were witched we might could beat him, put the pain back on what witched him. But I don't like to try that, him weak as he is."

Carpen' Jim hunched his shoulders down like a bear, making himself small. "Talking of witches. There's the holler woman. She's done good turns, ain't she? Way back? Some folk could run down yonder branch and ask?"

"She ain't come up out of there in years and years," Nora said. "And nobody's seen her 'n as long. Don't give the girl false hope. Anna, we'll take him down to Bill's cabin, put him to bed there. He can't be all the way up here like this."

Anna stared at her, dull. "You can't take him."

"You can't care for him yourself," Nora said. "Not as he needs it now. We'll settle him, and send for you—"

"You can't take him!"

"We'll take him," Nora said, and her eyes were root-hard now, set. "And that's all there is to it. Stay here, Anna. Sleep. You're rode hard, an' you can't help him."

Two men got their arms around Tom, pulling his elbows over their necks. They carried him out, the strange word muttering from his slack lips, and the crowd went after them, draining out of the room.

Milly put a hand on her neck and shook her head, pulling Anna to her feet and settling her on the bed. "She's right about sleep," she said, quiet. "Lie a while, and come down then."

She did not lie down. All the rest of the day, Anna sat on that bed, the empty room spinning around her, the walls distant, as if the air itself had thickened and bent the light. People came up now and then and knocked on the door, carrying plates and condolences, offers of help.

Through it all Anna sat and stared at them, holding herself tight. And then they were gone and she was weeping, great choking sobs, the tears hot in her eyes. She wept until the tears dried up, until her chest ached. Then she went out and sat on the porch and looked up at the darkening cliffs, Nora's words turning around in her head, over and over.

You can't help him.

No medicine, and no preacher. But there was something Tom had told her once after he'd brought her here, to this long valley filled with his kin: of the place down in the farthest branch, where the creek ran clear along a track that never grew over. A place nobody ever went, but everyone knew how to find. The witch holler.

She drew her shawl tight around her shoulders as she left the cabin, lantern in hand, her fingers twining in the tassels. Brush crunched and snapped under her feet. She followed the path down toward the nearest house, turned down a fork in the gloom, turned again at the next. Wind rasped in the branches, wooden claws scraping in the dark. Her breath fluttered in her throat.

"*Anna*," whispered a bat flying overhead on silent wings. "*Go back.*"

Anna only pulled the shawl tighter around her shoulders and went on. Three times she climbed, and three times she slid down the slick track, brush scratching her face. The way grew narrow and rutted as it wound across the slopes, jagged rocks thrusting up from the dirt. Finally she heard the rush of cold water tumbling through a crack in the rock.

Ducking under hanging boughs, she emerged onto the bottom

of the branch, the smell of mud and wet leaves thick in her nose. The lamplight glinted off a rolling current. A cabin perched above the water's edge; roof crumbling, the timbers warped and worn by countless spring melts, saplings growing through the broken windows. A tangle of ferns clawing up the walls. The door hung half off its hinges. Yet a light pulsed inside, weak as the embers of a dying fire. Something whispered on the air, prickling the hairs on the back of Anna's neck.

The boards sagged under her weight, groaning with rot as she went up onto the porch. Toads hopped away from her boots. The lamp blew out as she stepped through the hanging door. In its place flickered a dull red glow, rippling over the scatter of wood and broken shingles lying in the wet black dirt. Thin trunks stretched up into the gloom. A hunched form shifted on the other side of a slumbering fire.

"So," whispered a soft voice. "Anna O'Brien. I been waiting."

Slowly she sat by the fireside, the cold of the loam soaking up through her dress. "You know me?"

The wrinkled face considered her, round and deep-lined over a heavy blanket, the folds melting into dark. "I know many things. Some I hear. Some I'm told. I know your grandmother took a Cherokee man, and your father a Cherokee woman. I know that Anna Kinona took Tom O'Brien for husband. And I know something terrible's befallen him."

"What?" Anna said, her breath catching. "He screamed his own voice away. Can't speak for nonsense. Is he… is he witched?"

"Not witched. Not haint-touched. Worse."

"Worse how?"

The witch looked down at the fire, her eyes glinting. "There are old powers in the mountains," she said. "Old hills and old forests, and things that walked before all the peoples of man. Understand that? Some the people bargained with, and some they fought, drove out. But other men came and pushed them out, too. And all those old things, those strange things… they stayed. And sometimes, they crept back."

"But what's this got to do with—"

"*Listen.* In the far-off days, when Tanasi was new, the people who settled here encountered a thing of terror, a spirit of madness. A mind eater. It came at night from beneath the cliffs. No warrior could stand before it, and no hunter could escape it, for it drank their dreams and left them mad and foaming, screaming its name."

"Ewah?" Anna whispered.

The witch nodded, the movement ghostly in the gloom. "The medicine people sent a young woman with a totem of great power to bind it, drive it back beneath the cliffs for good. She was the Spirit-Talker, the Home-Protector. Running like a deer. But that… was long ago. The world has changed. Too much blood has been spilled beneath the rocks, and it has pushed its way back in."

Anna pulled her shawl tighter around her arms. "Can you save him?'

"The holler people are right, Anna O'Brien." A skeletal arm emerged and poked a stick into the fire. "Go home. There's nothing left to save."

Something cracked inside her, almost spilled her down out of the fog, down into cold despair. But then anger boiled up and she clung to it, forced it over her like a blanket. "No."

"No?" The witch leaned forward into the dim light, spiderweb shadows crawling across her dark face. "Your husband needs you, Anna. Will you leave him, now that he is not the strong young hunter you married?"

"I can't abandon him—"

"Then go. Warn the people that the Ewah walks."

"*No,*" Anna said. "I can't abandon him. But it has to be stopped."

"How will you stop it? The Ewah cannot die. It fears neither rifle nor knife, nor salt, silver or the word of God. You cannot revenge yourself on it. You will never see a drop of its blood spilled. And even if you drive it off, it will cost you dearly."

"It has!" Anna said. "And I can't— it *can't* cost any more. They're Tom's people up there in the holler. What about them? What happens when the devil comes for them? I can't sit by for that! You have to tell me what to *do*!"

Embers guttered in the firepit, shining on the mud. The rush of the creek filled the silence, tumbling and cold over the rocks.

"To banish the Ewah," the witch said, soft, "you need power, and power is a strange thing. Some you have. Some you have to trade for. A price higher, perhaps, than you wish to pay."

"I'll pay it."

Black eyes considered her in the dark. Then a gnarled hand slid forward, clutching a strange shape, a tangle of shadow over the fire. Anna reached out and took it, hesitant. Brittle fur brushed against her fingers. As she turned it over, red light glinted off carved wood and old hide, stretched out into a snarling face. A tingle ran in prickling spirals up her arm.

"What is it?"

"The one thing I can give you," said the witch. In the firepit, the embers flared. "The Wampus Mask. Woven from wildcat hide and sinew by a true medicine man of the *Aniyunwiya*, called *Tsalagi*, called Cherokee. This will hide you from the spirit's gaze. Go up under the cliffs tonight. Leave your lamp behind. Stare into the Ewah's eyes and you are lost. Let it catch you and you are lost. But it fears the thing in your hand, fears it more than anything. Surprise it first… and maybe you'll live to tell of it."

Anna unwound her shawl and wrapped the mask in its folds. "Thank you."

"Wait." Fingers cold as bone seized her arm. "Do not step foot on this path unless you'll walk it to the end. Wherever it takes you."

"If that's what needs doing," Anna said, pulling her hand free. She stood up fast, stepped out of the door frame and into the night, the red glow dwindling into the darkness.

She went swiftly now, stumbled back up the slope, one hand outstretched to guide her along the tree trunks. Moonlight filtered down through the leaves, a faint silver shine on the rocks. The chatter of insects pulsed on the humid air. Three times up and three times down, and then a fourth scramble up onto the valley path, breath husky in her throat, until her cabin swam out of the gloom, sitting dark and alone at the top of the holler.

She left the lantern on the porch and paused, thinking of Tom down in the valley somewhere, curled and quaking in a bed. "*Go back*," crooned an owl diving on a mouse. It pinned its prey in cruel talons and drifted away into the dark. "*Go back, Anna O'Brien.*"

"Not yet," Anna said. She took one last look at the cabin and then, mouth set, she waded into the forest.

It was rough going. The trees grew like towers over the underbrush, boughs blotting out the moon. Logs lay scattered and moldering over the broken ground. Several times Anna tripped and fell, or snagged her dress on sharp limbs, the fabric giving way with rips that sounded loud as gunshots in her ears. Finally, she ducked down behind the buttress roots of a great tree and ripped half the dress off. Tying the fabric around her waist, she tucked the mask into her makeshift belt, the air chilly across her bare knees.

Onward through the undergrowth, throat tight, hands up as if they could somehow lighten her tread. The ground grew rockier, moonlit shafts pouring down through the clearings. Ahead the trees thinned out at the base of midnight cliffs, a field of jagged boulders and gullies, leaning pine snags painted in faint daubs of silver.

"*Beware*," hissed a copperhead coiled in a rotting log. "*Beware…*"

The drone of insects cut out. Anna froze, listening to the clack of dead branches, holding a hand over her mouth to muffle her breath. A prickle of invisible legs inched over her flesh. The air turned in against her tongue, squirming and slick. Something stirred in the high cracks on the rock faces, a glimpse of shadows stretching out over the pitted stone, dark spears flowing out of the crevices. Gone even as she turned her head.

The crawling sensation grew, a thousand invisible insects digging into her skin. Out in the trees, a heavy footfall echoed on the slope.

Squeezing against the nearest boulder, Anna unwrapped the mask with shaking fingers and slipped it on. The dry hide and wood molded itself against her face, fever hot; something snapped behind her ears. The crawling sensation slipped away as she gulped at the chill air. The night was brighter, rocks picked out in silver light; dead trees towered on all sides, white and brittle, split by whirling shadows. Bushes clustered against slabs of broken sandstone.

The footsteps rolled over the boulders. With each impact the mask throbbed, the heat growing until it was nearly scalding. Approaching, but from which direction? She shrank against the sandstone.

The sounds stopped. Something sniffed, a whistling inhalation of breath.

"I smell you out there in the dark," said the Ewah. The syllables dripped out, one by one, slow as the last blood running off a carcass. "I've fat myself on white man's mind, this night past, and I am sated. Run, little girl. Run and I will let you go undrunk."

Anna's flesh crawled. She should run, run until her bones broke, until the branches tore open ribbons of her flesh, until she could lock herself away in the cabin and never again go out into the black forest. Instead she drew in a quiet, shuddering breath, squeezing her fingers tight into the rock. Leaning around the boulder, she stared out over the slope. Even with the aid of the mask, she saw nothing but long straight trunks and tangles of dead trees beneath the cliff face.

"Stay, then." The Ewah's chuckle bubbled on the air. "You have the blood in you. Blood like I have not smelled in long, long years. Not since I left my favorite people to go beneath the stone. I miss them so…"

Anna gritted her teeth, sweat trickling down her forehead. Long bands of shadow tangled across her vision. She saw nothing. And yet the voice was so close, almost as if it were right on top of her—

The thought coiled in her mind. Slowly, she looked up.

The shadowy forest before her shifted and moved. It resolved out of the space between the trees, a man-shape spindly and thin as the trunks, its head ducking beneath the high branches. A leg stretched over her head, black against the cold stars. She stared as the long silhouette passed above her, laying a clawed hand atop the boulder as it went. It crouched on the other side, spindly arms folded against its sides, teeth glinting in a grinning skull.

It hadn't seen her. It had stepped right over her, staring with its white eyes, and yet it had never looked down. Anna brought a hand to the mask and felt it throb against her fingers. Her limbs were leaden with terror, her breath sobbing behind her clenched jaw. It hadn't seen her. But the size of it, huge and gnarled—how could she hope to frighten that? What had she been thinking, coming here?

"You're here somewhere," the Ewah said. Its head cocked like a heron, glancing over the boulder. Claws scraped into the sandstone. A

deep grinding rasp, a cracking of rock; Anna shoved herself away, ducking her head against the whirling white eyes, and darted for the nearest tree. Bracken crashed behind her as the boulder tore loose from the soil, rolling down the slope.

"Quick, wherever you are. Why scuttle, little mouse? Little girl? Come out. Let me have a look at you. Let us be… civilized."

Anna slid around a pine trunk, stepping over rotten branches, and ran over a ridge of sandstone. Behind her an elongated pale hand came creeping across the rocks, fingers questing. Slipping under a leaning snag, she squeezed behind the overhang of another boulder. She had to go, now, before it found her. If she got to the deep trees, maybe she could vanish into the dark, slip down the mountain—

Something soft buckled under her feet. She bent down and picked up a battered, broad-brimmed hat, the side crushed where she'd stepped on it. Tom's hat. A piece of him torn away and abandoned in the trees.

"I smell the white man on you, girl. His mind screams still in my stomach." The Ewah rose on its haunches, jaws working. Shining eyes swept back and forth over the forest. "He screamed so loud, so loud, and tasted so sweet. Such a horror I made of him. But I was kind and sent him back. Did you like that?"

Anna's heartbeat roared inside her, roaring over the fear, hard and hot as the mask on her face. Her fingers dug into her palms, locking Tom's hat in an iron grip. It wanted her to run, to drive her screaming down the mountain. No running.

"I tire of your rudeness," hissed the voice, probing out over the hillside. "I think I am hungry after all. I think I will sniff you out, wherever you are. I think I will make you run… "

"You ran once, didn't you?"

The words were out of her mouth before Anna could snatch them back. Her eyes widened. She heard the air whistle, heard it and sprinted away up the slope, shoving herself down behind a deadfall. Behind her the stone exploded into dust under a slapping hand.

"Run? I do not run. I went back under the stone—"

"Of your own accord?"

"Where are you?" the Ewah snarled. Its head swung back and forth on its long neck, arms searching, hands questing. Trunks bent and cracked as it pulled them over, rocks rolling down the hill as it yanked them from the soil. Anna flitting from tree to tree, keeping at its back, eyes down, the mask picking out a silver way through the scree.

"Afraid?"

"I am fear!" The Ewah's voice was a howl. "Back into a new world, back to the thunder of falling trees and hot blood spilled beneath the rocks. The medicine people are gone and I am free, free to walk a fearful land that does not know me. Free to sup minds and children's dreams! The cat-face is gone! The running deer is gone! What is left in the world to protect you from me? *Come out!*"

"You want me to come out?" Anna called, her voice cracking. She stepped out onto the open slope behind it, fists balled. Stepped out, breathed, and closed her eyes. "Then *turn*."

She heard it rather than saw it. Heard the Ewah whirling, white eyes roiling, hissing through jagged teeth. Heard it find not a soft frightened girl, not prey, but the burning eyes of the Wampus Mask.

White heat pierced Anna's skull. An ear-splitting shriek echoed off the cliffs. She opened her eyes in time to see the Ewah rear back, claws swiping in agony and terror, and stumble into a stand of dying trees. It rolled, scrabbling as far away as it could on its spindly legs, gouging deep furrows into rock and soil as it fled toward the cracks in the cliff face. For a moment it was a flat thing, wriggling like a spider. And then it was gone, only the echo of its scream lingering on the dark.

Anna picked herself up, her hands shaking. The wind gusted over the slope, cool against the tatters of her dress. Then she rocked back on her heels and laughed, a laugh that howled out of her like the wind. "Run!" she screamed. Heat shot through her, spiraling through her limbs. "Run, goddamn you! And don't you come back!"

Triumphantly, she reached up and snatched the mask off her face.

A blinding flash of heat boiled across her skin. The world tilted. She looked up from the ground, at the shadows and moonlight spinning, rolled over and retched. Blood in her mouth. She had to stand up. Thunder in her ears. A foot digging at the ground as she tried to rise. She had to stand up…

Then the world was a dark sea, sucking her down.

***

Three days after she made the trade, Anna O'Brien woke in her bed. She surfaced slowly, to butter-yellow sunlight pooling on the linens and glowing on the grey log walls, rich against the colors of quilt and wall hanging. The shutters were thrown open, warm air slack against her face. Her limbs ached, scratches and bruises carving their jagged ways over her tan arms. When had she gotten those? Why did her left side feel so light?

She frowned, pushed herself up on weak elbows. Looked down at the rumple of quilt before her, at the shallow fold where her memory said her left leg should be, and her eyes swore it was not. Numb, uncomprehending, she slid her hand over the thigh, fumbling past the knee for the calf, the foot. Her left heel was throbbing, pressing into the mattress. But there was nothing. Nothing at all.

Tears prickled in her eyes. She squeezed the quilt in her fist, squeezed it until her knuckles hurt, and drew in a long breath, letting it out as slowly as she could. Her throat felt raw. She tore her gaze away, taking in the sunlit cabin, taking in anything but the stump under the covers, and stopped.

"Tom?"

He was standing there by the side of the bed, his hands in the pockets of his trousers, looking down at her with concerned eyes. Beard soft and brown on his plain, crooked face. His hat and tattered hunting jacket hung behind him on the chair. When he saw her looking, he smiled and sat down. She stared at him, heart pounding, drinking him in: the blue of his eyes, his strong hands. A giddy light raced through her chest, made her hands tremble under the quilt. Her head spun. Birdsong filtered through the windows like gentle music on the breeze.

The cabin door creaked. Milly and another woman came in from the porch, talking in low tones. Anna had a glimpse of Nora out there, her shoulders shaking against Carpen' Jim, the big man looking bewildered. Then Milly ushered the other woman out and shut the door.

"Milly?" Anna said.

Milly whirled, sagging in relief. She picked up a tin cup off the table and came over, sitting on the side of the bed. "Thank God. Oh, thank god. How're you feeling?"

The water was a cold balm against Anna's lips. She drank the cup dry and sighed. "Bad. How'd I…"

"I got worried about you is what happened," Milly said. "Came to bring you down to see him and you were gone. And then there was all that awful noise on the rocks at night, right terrible sounds. Woke everybody up. Carpen' Jim and John and some others went up under the cliffs in the morning to see what had happened, and you were just lying there, cold. Some devil mask in your hand. Dress all ripped up and not hardly breathing. Looked like someone had kicked the slope up and kicked you, too."

"I feel… kicked," Anna said. "My leg?"

"Carpen' Jim said it was mel—" Milly screwed her face up. "It was gone, anyway. He smashed that mask in your hand and you started breathing again. You been asleep since. Three days. Had us worried sick, Anna. What were you doing up there?"

"Went to see the witch down in the holler. Got the mask from her and settled with what hurt him. Won't be coming back."

Milly nodded, her eyes wide and uncomprehending. "Well. Don't you worry about the leg. Carpen' John's working you up a new one out of oak, like he did back after the war. He's right good at that, I reckon. Won't that be nice?"

"It'll do," Anna said. She forced herself to keep looking at Tom's eyes, clinging to them.

"Now don't be short, Anna." Milly's worried eyes flicked to the chair. "You can polish it and all. Reckon you'll look right smart with it."

"I can get by," Anna put a smile on her face. "I'll get by. How's he up and about? Did you bring him up?"

Milly followed her gaze. "Who?"

The silence stretched for a long, terrible moment. Tom shifted and

Anna stared at him, at the chair and its empty shadow, the shapes of the hat and coat blue and alone at the floor. The room pulsed, a slow dance of light from the swaying branches outside, too bright on her eyes, keeping time to the pounding of her heartbeat. "Tom," she said, and looked back at Milly, a cold blade of dread sliding into her stomach. "He's right…"

But she knew, even before she saw the look on the other woman's face.

"How long?" Anna whispered.

"They buried him last night, Anna." Milly's eyes were wet. "He shook himself out the night before we found you. Didn't wake up. We tried to wake you 'fore we laid him down, tried real hard, but you wouldn't— I thought we'd lose you too. I didn't want to say straight off. I'm so sorry."

No tears. No screaming. No pain. She felt only a curious numbness as she lay against the sheets, her hand grasping the quilt as she stared at the chair. It was all happening to someone else. Someone with one leg, someone with no husband. Not her. Not Anna O'Brien.

"Thank you," she said quietly. "Please go."

"Sure." Milly stood and smoothed her hands on her skirt. "Sure. I'll… be on the porch. With the others."

Anna heard the door close, wood rattling against the frame. She looked around at the cabin Tom had built her, one year ago, when he took her down into Tennessee from higher mountains, took her here and promised her a home, and at the man who'd built it, staring at her, so whole and real she ached to hold him, ached to scold him, ached to kiss him. Ached. Closing her eyes, she swallowed.

"You should go too," she said, and breathed out.

When she opened her eyes, the cabin was empty. A chair sat before her, his battered hat and torn coat hanging from one side. Spindly wood and beaten fabric. Nothing more.

***

That night Anna dreamed again of black waters lapping beneath the stone, deep and cold and bottomless. She sank down into them and was back in the witch's cabin, sitting by a fire as embers whirled and danced in the dark. Frogs chirped and whirred in the rafters. The saplings swayed, vanishing up into the night. "I told you there would be a price," said the witch, watching her from across the flames. "Perhaps more than you wanted."

"Did you know?" Anna said. Her hands rested on her legs, and her left leg was wooden beneath her fingers.

"Did I know? Of course I knew. I knew the day I first placed it on my head and went up from Tanasi to face the mind-drinker, an age and an age ago. Running like a deer. Spirit-Talker. Home-protector." The firelight caught the witch's face, and for the briefest of moments the only thing there was bone. "I have waited here long years, ground down by rivers of time. I saw our people grow, and I saw them go where I could not follow. Down all the turning seasons I waited. And when I saw you, Anna Kinona—"

"O'Brien." Anna's voice snapped out, cold in the dark. "It's Anna O'Brien."

"—I knew you'd be able to pay the price."

Twigs crackled and popped in the firepit. "I've paid it."

"Not yet," whispered the witch. "You lost a love, though he was lost to you before ever you took up the mask. You lost a leg, and that was what you traded. But the price? You'll pay that all your life. You might have left your husband. You might have lived a different fate. Now you are here. The price of medicine magic is medicine magic. The price is seeing trouble and being bound to fix it. You'll walk again, Anna O'Brien. But you'll never be able to walk away."

"I can't," Anna said. "I—the mask is smashed."

"Power is a strange thing." Twisted hands spread up, knucklebones shining dimly. "Some you have to trade for. Some you have. *You* heard the whispers of the voiceless. *You* stopped the pale demon with your courage and saved your husband's people, though they'll never know it. The mask was the knife in your hand, it's true. But yours was the hand. And there is so much work to be done."

The fire licked up and out across the shingles. Cool against her wooden leg. "What work?"

"Hard times coming," the witch whispered. "Can't you feel it? The devouring of all things, tract by tract, hill by hill, tree by tree. Marching the *Aniyunwiya* first. Marching everyone out next. The old compacts are broken, and dark things are squeezed from dark and bloody ground. Who will face them, Spirit-Talker?"

Anna was silent a long time. "I don't know how."

"You'll learn."

"No," Anna said. Even in the dream she shuddered. "I mean, I don't—How can I—"

The witch's face was unreadable in the gloom. Then a hand reached out over the dying flames, a young hand. It took Anna's and squeezed. "Did you see him?"

Anna nodded, not trusting herself to speak.

"Hold on to that," said the witch. The coals flickered out, one by one, and the shadows stole in. "Hold on to him. Carry him with you. And then, when you walk the moonlit road with a wooden leg and the spirits at your back, you can remember why you paid the price. And you can stop others from suffering a fate like his."

A light glared in the firepit. The cabin melted into nothing, saplings spiraling into columns of mist. In the glow she saw a woman, battered hat pulled low over clear grey eyes, hunting jacket flapping soundlessly in the wind. Spectral things pressed about her, clawing and biting, and shrank back as blue fire rippled along her hands. The woman looked up, and in the dying flicker of light, Anna saw herself.

The glow dissolved. The last coal dwindled and died. The dream faded into the dark.

"Can you do that?" called the faint echo of the witch's voice as she opened her eyes.

"Yes," said Anna O'Brien, though the room was empty and there was no one there to listen. "I think maybe I can."

HOLLOW KNOWLEDGE
1900-1901

So many things to know.

Anna O'Brien picked them up as she went, dressed in a broad-brimmed hat and a hunting coat and trousers, collecting scraps of knowledge like she'd collected fabrics for a quilt, like she plucked poultice plants for her satchel. She pushed all else away. *You'll learn*, she'd been told in a dream that was not a dream, and it had been less a promise than a command. Learn, or you won't be able to do the things you've set out to do. Learn it all, everything you can, and know you'll be learning all the days of your life.

***

The first thing to learn was her new leg. Carpen' John knew his business. He'd measured it to her and fit it well, a Hanger-style leg fashioned of whittled-down barrel staves, hinged at the foot to help her walk. But there were challenges. Her left leg throbbed and ached where there was no leg to throb and ache, often soft, sometimes in sharp stabbing pains that left her gasping. Wearing the wooden leg for too long hurt. Sometimes she settled herself down on a log and took it off, sat long enough that she forgot, until she went to stand up and spilled herself on the dirt. There were days she woke and looked at her wooden foot and raged quietly, her fists clenching against the ground, days she hated it, days she couldn't bear to walk for long. She missed her leg as much sometimes as she missed him, and sometimes more. A ghost she couldn't settle.

Learning to walk meant learning how hard the road was. Seventeen years of household chores—fetch the water, carry the firewood, beat the quilts—had made her strong, but now she was walking on one leg, leaning on a walking stick as she went. Every day, learning how to walk. Aches ground deep into her bones; her flesh grew taut over ropy muscle. At night she slept in open fields or crept into stranger's barns, or did as Tom had done on long hunting trips, dragging branches and logs over the root-ball of a fallen tree, stuffing the bottom with leaves before wiggling inside. She got by on edible plants, fistfuls of berries when she came across them, fruit pocketed from unwatched orchards, the occasional rabbit and possum raided from someone else's snares. Eventually she simply undid a set of cord traps in the woods, unwinding them and rolling them in her bag. Better that one small theft than the constant thieving.

Learning the road meant learning to talk, and talking was a struggle. She had always been serious, had always been quiet. Now she found herself retreating atop a high hill of silence, slipping off the path when she heard oncoming footsteps, lurking at the edge of general stores and small towns, watching the people pass with a hungry intensity. Trying to work out what to say and how to say it, she often said nothing, and cursed herself for her silence. How was she going to learn if she couldn't ask who she should learn from? But a panic seized her when she tried, a terrible awareness of her wooden leg, the strangeness of what she was asking for, the fact of her threadbare trousers and work shirt. To speak, she'd have to explain, and what she had to say was inexplicable, impossible for her to articulate, even to herself. Easier not to speak at all.

And yet there was Elaine Ferner, a granny-woman in the woods outside of Sylva who worked through her near-speechlessness early on. She was short and hefty, with a snub nose and eyes that disappeared in the wrinkles of her face when she smiled. Anna came upon her digging ginseng in a creek bottom, sat and watched her, and jumped when the woman looked up and called her down. Anna stayed by Elaine a week, sleeping on the floor and going out with the older woman by day into the streams and muddy hills, leaning sometimes on her shoulder. The granny-woman talked all the while, rattling out plant names and properties, and smacking Anna lightly on the head when they found the right flower, the right leaf, the right root.

"Remember," she would say, and Anna managed to keep most of it. Yellowroot and sassafras in a compress for stings, cuts and burns; feverwort to bring down swelling; catnip tea for cramping; and the quiet edibles of the forest, ramps and papaws, wood chicken mushrooms, black walnuts. Medicine ways.

She began to pry herself open. She asked for hospitality, and paid it back by carrying messages down the branches and hollers. When she heard movement on the road she stood and waited for whoever was coming, peddler or preacher or family bound for flatland markets, and she forced herself to talk with all of them. She'd lost too much time to silence. Now, when people asked what she was doing out on the road, she took a breath and told them she was learning. Asked what she was learning, she told them she was learning magic.

Most knew nothing of that. But some knew people who did. Addie Brown—handsome, her white apron and calico dress stark against her dark skin— knew something of the dead, and she welcomed Anna inside her narrow house in a freedman settlement on the Carolina line, as the neighbors watched in guarded silence. There Addie recalled her mother's stories of working in the big house, back before the war: haints glimpsed out in the fields at night, rising with the new moon and standing out in the grass, staring at the house or pressing on the doors to the slave quarters, waiting for someone to let them in. A haint couldn't hurt you directly, Addie said, but it could scare the life out of you, torment you into running and harming yourself that way. Might be they could toss you around some, too. Some folk had the lord's power in them, the power to breathe ghosts out or whistle them away. For everyone else there was salt or sulphur, laid out over a threshold or sprinkled on a grave.

"Why salt?" Anna said.

"It's a pure thing, ain't it?" Addie said. "It scours. Keeps what's good, good, an' drives out the bad. It's a good thing to have 'round in any case. You can't go wrong with salt."

For a month in late summer she went with Jubal Herricks, a stringy man with wild eyes who claimed the Lord's power to beat the black arts. She found him a drunk and a letch, and a font of dubious remedies. The signs of witchcraft were clear to Jubal; an old woman or man cast out and living alone, ugliness and infirmity, unnatural dark skin like the Melungeon people had, or witchmarks where the devil liked to suckle like a baby at the teat. Witches made themselves out of spite and meanness, he told Anna. They made black bargains with the devil in the woods, danced and rutted with him, and fashioned poisoned witch-balls to curse and kill. Take nothing from a witch, and give them nothing but a lashing when you found them, hot irons, or death from a heart drawn on a holly tree, with a spike driven into it every day for nine days. Besides that, salt for skin-changers and hags, and silver for all of them.

Mostly useless. But some of it was good sense; the rules of giving and not giving, the signs of curse by witch-ball, and salt and silver. These Anna committed to memory, along with other tricks and half-remembered cures picked up from those she met. A warming charm; the numbers three, nine and thirteen for breaking spells; wild horseradish slipped under the pillow for nightmares and ghost-ridings. The way of lost things, an insect sealed in a little bottle with secret words, its buzzing against the glass pointing like a compass to anything mislaid.

Magic was hard work. Harder than walking, harder even than talking. Using power left Anna feeling drained and light-headed. Still, she began to practice in small ways. She settled ghosts, tangling them up in her inhalation and breathing them out, then scattering a bit of salt from a pouch she kept in her bag for good measure. She threw herself against a hag in the backwoods—salt on an empty skin, long limbs, wild eyes full of hate—and barely escaped with her life.

She sat outside the hag's cabin after the body stopped twitching, bone weary, her face in her hands. The pain in her head slowed, melted back into the usual stew of weariness, until all she felt were her teeth, clenched tight in an aching jaw. Her hands weren't trembling. When had that happened?

She looked up and sighed, her breath pluming on the air. Beyond the hills, the far horizon glowed.

***

Onward. Through small villages tucked up in the cove valleys, tiny footbridges over little creeks, near-vertical fields of corn. Her first clear-cut slope, glimpsed from another hill over, as though a dress had been torn from the body of the earth, leaving it bare and bleeding under the hugeness of the sky, so that she slept badly for nights afterward. Mountains rising above the canopies like the spine of the world, wreathed in wisps of milk-white cloud or blue smoke. Goldenrod and skunk smell in the woods; red and gold leaves come September, spinning around her as she walked, tugged loose and set adrift on the tumbling breeze. Whispers from the birds in the trees. The creaking of wagon wheels on rock. Nooses on gnarled trees. Cattle moving through the forest, plucking the green leaves from the ground, hulking against the saplings. The first tang of winter in her nose.

The clothing settled on her back, the coat and its many pockets, the hat keeping the sun off, shading her eyes, the sensation of trouser cloth on her thighs fading. So many things to know. So much hollow knowledge. She learned, and kept on.

NIGHT ON THE BALD

1901

There was nothing, Anna O'Brien decided, she wouldn't give for a fire.

Evening washed over the ridgeline trail, painting the surrounding slopes the dull grey of old metal. The wind cut against the sparse forest, whirling around thin tree trunks and thickets, setting the birch branches rattling. There was no escape from it; even with her battered coat pulled tight around her, the chill crept in, freezing Anna's limbs, making the fitting of her wooden leg ache. It was a bad time to be out on the road.

She tucked herself tighter against the fallen log, put her hands against her mouth and exhaled. Her breath slid easily through the ratty gloves, the bitter air plucking the warmth away. For a moment she thought longingly of the abandoned town at the bottom of the slope. If she hadn't been so damn stubborn, she could be down there now, warming her hands in one of those empty cabins, listening to the frustrated wind blow through the walls. If she'd just overlooked the overturned furniture, the crockery sitting in the cupboards, bed after bed with mold-spackled sheets…

Anna hugged her knees against her chest, her mouth a thin line. Cold bark pressed against her back. She had stood at the crossroads and looked at the houses, open doorways standing dark in the wan fields. Only the ridge road had been clear of buildings; she'd followed it as fast as she'd dared, thighs smarting from the climb, resentful of her own stiffness and eager to put that desolate place behind her. Only when she saw the sun setting over the mountains did it occur to her that she'd made a mistake. By then it was too late to do anything about it; too late to do anything but duck down and think about what to do next.

Hugging her coat tighter around her body, she gritted her teeth against the ache in her foot. Branches clacked overhead. Sharp wind whirled around her, burning cold against her cheeks. Leaves tumbled past over the rocky ground.

The hell with it. She'd have to find herself a place for the night, and that meant she had to move. Taking a deep breath, she twisted one hand over another, and closed her eyes. Prickles of heat gathered in her stomach. Concentrating, she moved her hand again. The prickles became a warm current, spiraling down her arms and wafting up the tips of her fingers. This time as she exhaled, the warmth flared all over her body–and stayed.

The world spun. Closing her eyes, she tilted her head back and swallowed, fighting through the dizziness that always came with conjuring. The first time she'd tried the charm, she'd nearly passed out. The second, her leg gave and tumbled her down a hillside. But it was getting better, wasn't it? She just had to keep going. Keep pushing. It had taken her months to get used to walking, the day after she woke to find her leg gone. Why should magic come any easier?

Anna caught her breath and sighed, pushing herself up. Pulling her hat down against the wind, she picked her way forward, the tapping of her stick jarring her numb fingers. Moss crunched under her feet. The warming charm blunted the force of the wind, at least a bit, but it wouldn't last. Maybe there would be an outcrop somewhere, a fallen tree large enough to tuck herself under on the ridgeside. Enough dry leaves to scrape into a bed.

The wind stuttered. For the briefest of moments the air hung flat and heavy over the ridge. Anna stopped: A soft weight had fallen on her, like the warning touch of a spiderweb stretched across the trail. Something watching. But she saw nothing amid the quaking branches and the black strips of shadow swaying on the stones. Nothing but random scraps of moonlight, and in the space between them–

Anna froze, the breath catching in her throat.

On the trail beside her was a dog.

It stood dark against the pale birch trees, its shoulders tall as Anna's waist, its back and flanks a matted tangle of black fur. Huge paws sprouted from the leaf litter. Its heavy-jawed head studied her, round eyes glowing a pale blue. When she met its gaze the dog moved, long legs sweeping soundlessly over the uneven ground. It drifted up the trail and stopped a little way up the ridgeline, swinging back to look at her, ears pricked.

Anna's fingers gripped her walking stick. Standing there she was a little girl again, huddling under the blanket next to her mother and sister after a night of tales, the forests of her mind swarming with stories of the ghost-eater, who haunted lonely roads and lurked under lynching trees. The black dog. The shadow in the shape of a hound.

"What do you want?" she said.

Dried leaves swirled through the dog's frame, catching faint glimmers of blue from the shining eyes. Its gaze never wavered.

"Do I follow you? Is that it?"

The ears flicked. In a languid movement the dog was up on its feet and gone, the gloom folding swallowing it up. It stepped out from behind a tree several feet away and stared, head cocked. Fear and curiosity fought inside Anna for a long moment. Finally, she took a deep breath, the cold biting into her teeth.

"All right," she said. "Let's go."

The black dog stalked forward again, and this time Anna O'Brien followed. Brush and heather crunched under her boots, snatching at the coarse fabric of her trousers. She kept her free hand stretched forward, guiding herself from tree to spindly tree, the trunks withered and wind-curled under her gloved fingers. Her shoulder ached from the weight of the bag. Sweat gathered in clammy beads beneath her hat.

Then the trees fell away. The ridgeline expanded into a sloping bald, a vast clearing of gnarled underbrush and tufts of pale grass. No trees grew thereon the vast clearing, and no high rhododendrons bushes or tall thickets of lilac. The wind ran fast and hard, waves rippling through the stems, as if the hillside field were running. Running, and going nowhere. Ahead, dark against the moonlit clouds, stood the ruined timbers of a church.

Perhaps the carpenters who'd raised it had originally produced a tall, straight building, with firm joints and a steady, dignified face. If so, that had been long ago. Now the walls sagged, the timbers subtly out of true, as if some great weight had warped them out from the inside. Spars projected up from the half-collapsed rooftop like ribs. The steeple tower looked as if it had been chewed by enormous jaws. Under the wind, at the faint reaches of Anna's hearing, came a distant thrum of sound.

She came to a halt, adjusting her coat. The dog hung back as well. It paced, head sweeping back and forth over the ground. The night swallowed it up and spat it out on a ripple of exposed stone, its great body curving like a bow as it stared at the church.

"What's here?" Anna said. Her voice came out quiet, barely audible over the rustle of the grass. "What're you after?"

The dog turned back to look at her, teeth glinting in its open jaws. Its black coat twisted into nothingness. The blue embers of its eyes winked out.

Anna waited for it to reemerge, to give her some further sign. But the field lay empty under the stars, and gradually she understood. She was alone.

She shivered, a wash of cold air licking her face. The church loomed against the dark, a weird, flickering light pouring from the high windows. Muffled whispers scraped faintly against her ears. There was something about the place that reminded her of the cabins below the ridgeline, of black doors and rooms full of everything but people. But the warmth of her conjuring was wearing off, nibbled away by the chill and her physical exertion, and a chatter built in her teeth. Whatever waited for her inside, at least she'd be out of the wind.

Scraps of wood littered the grass outside the church front. Anna picked her way through the debris and paused at the heavy door. It alone seemed in good repair, and as she put a hand out to touch it she heard the faint sound of voices through the frame. She glanced over her shoulder at the empty bald, looking at the distant treeline. Then, taking a deep breath, she brought her fist up and knocked three times against the wood.

Hinges creaked. The door shuddered open in a wash of red light, revealing the backlit shape of a heavyset woman standing in the entryway. Behind her, Anna glimpsed rows of benches and broken chairs.

"Well, come in," said the woman. "No call to stand about."

Anna blinked. "Thank you."

The woman ushered her inside. A small crowd of people sat near the door, their faces indistinct in the dim light. Only the closest seats were filled; the rest ran in empty lines all the way to the far end of the church, where the pews had been ripped out and piled carelessly along the walls. A low fire licked sluggishly at the floorboards, casting an eerie glow against the walls. Red light washed across the uneven planks. The absence of wind cheered Anna in some small way; the click of the latch thudding into place behind her did not. It took everything she had not to flinch.

"You're early, sister. We won't be getting started for a while yet."

"Didn't want to be late," Anna said. "Never… been before."

"I thought as much." The woman's eyes glittered out of a sturdy face. A much-patched dress and fine apron hung from her sloping shoulders. "I been coming long enough, and I never seen you. Where're you from?"

"Here and there." More faces were turning to look at her. Most of them were women, showing a range of ages–some of them as old and hard-beaten, others as young as Anna herself, or younger. At first glance they all looked normal, even pleasant, but the more she stared the more unease fluttered in her gut. "I been walking the hills some. Drifting."

"That's good. Nothing tying you down, and easy to move on when you've had your fill." The stout woman smiled, her eyes disappearing in a mass of wrinkles, and patted her belly. "My wandering days are done, sister. That's a young girl's game. Some year'll come when you want a roof over your head and steady food. You got a name?"

"Anna."

"I'm Kezia. Pleased to know you."

Anna flashed a smile across her face, taking in the sagging benches around her. Her eyes were drawn to the fire, and what lay just beyond: a crude altar brooding on a base of carved stone, constructed out of woven branches and the remnants of the pulpit. A trio of raven skulls sat at the top, firelight flickering on their painted beaks. The stars were cold pinpricks through the holes in the roof.

"Emptier than I thought it'd be," Anna said.

"Oh, Hollow Jenny and the rest will be along," said a woman at a nearby bench. She looked about Anna's age, her long legs crossed, knees poking out from beneath her short cotton dress. "Whenever they decide to stir themselves, anyhow."

"You hush," said an old man. "Jenny moves on her own time and you know it. Always has."

Kezia shrugged. "Been coming later and later. Mary's right about that."

"But she does come. She's been in a mood, that's all. Haven't you seen?"

"Oh, we all seen it," Kezia said. "Her wrinkles are spreading fast now, aren't they? Faster with her sharing her take like the rest of us. She'll be switching soon, I guess."

A few lips pursed at that. Mary hunched over at her seat, her slender fingers digging into her elbows. Curling her body up on the pew like she was trying to hide inside it. She studied Anna from beneath a fringe of matted hair. "How'd you hear of the gathering, then?"

She'd been expecting that question, and had her answer ready. "Huldah Jurgens made mention of it. Said I ought to go."

"I knew her," Kezia said.

Anna's heart beat very fast. "Knew her?"

"Huldah got herself salted sometime past," one of the women said, stretching. "That's what I hear. Some hag-breaker found her skin and laced it with salt and hot pepper. Burned her right up."

The memory of Huldah's snarling face swam up, and the twist in Anna's belly grew sharp. She'd forced herself to stand and watch, all those months ago, as the sunlight came through the windows and caught the wet body tearing at its poisoned flesh. And now that she recalled, hadn't there been an altar out behind Huldah's shack as well, a jagged pile of logs crowned with three raven skulls?

"Shame," Anna said. As casually as she could, she backed toward the door. "She taught me a fair bit before I went."

"Really? She never looked the teaching kind," said Kezia, lurching over to an empty pew. "Not a joining kind, either. Sour old frog. Didn't moisten my eyes much to hear of her passing, I must say."

"You *did* know her," Anna said. She felt the wood on her back. Her hands slid behind her, fumbling–

Keziah chuckled. "Just met her the once. I'm sure you'll fit in better. Oh, don't skulk so! You never know who'll come knocking. Come sit, girl. You must be tired."

Anna smiled at her and slipped her fingers off the latch. A cold draft rippled across her face as she stepped away from the door, and for a brief second she felt the weight of invisible eyes on the back of her neck. "It's been a long walk. I'm glad you sent the dog."

Keziah cocked her head. "The dog?"

"A black dog?" Without quite knowing why, she trailed a glove along the wall timbers as she walked to the nearest empty pew. Something roiled strangely beneath her gloves, rolling up her arm. She pulled her hand away.

"Oh, *him*." Kezia's voice was almost fond. "The ghost-eater. He knows there's food locked up in here, if he could get at it. He used to make a nuisance of himself till we taught him better. You just sit there and wait on Jenny to arrive. Won't be long now."

The low babble of conversation picked up, the crowd turning back to talk amongst themselves. Anna dropped her bag and walking stick onto the floor and leaned on the edge of the pew, listening to the creak of the rafters overhead. The low fire at the front of the room cast little heat. Even with her weight against the back of the bench she could feel her leg muscles starting to cramp.

What would happen if she tried to leave? She wasn't sure they knew Huldah's name, these people with their sunken faces and lidded eyes, and that meant nothing good. Witches at the least, and possibly worse. What would they do to her if they thought she didn't belong there? If they put her knowing Huldah's name together with the hag's fate? No, it was no use making another try for the door, even with Kezia back in conversation with the man next to her. Better to conjure herself another round of warmth and keep quiet.

She braced herself and concentrated, inhaling. The prickle leapt up into her arms immediately, as if it had been waiting to be called; a flood of heat pouring up inside her. Shrill whispers grew louder in her ears. Her stomach gave a little flip and she almost stopped, tried to stop, but the pressure was building in her limbs and it had to be let out. Her hands twisted of their own accord. The breath rushed from her lungs.

Her hands burst into flame.

She stumbled back off the pew with a yelp of surprise. The fire on her palms sprouted up as she hit the wall, snatching greedily at the air. Her gloves caught instantly, threads shriveling into glowing flakes of ash. Her arms burned like molten rivers inside her sleeves. The whispering exploded into a storm of screaming voices, the terrible wails buffeting her, forcing her down against the cold floorboards, and her fingers burned, burned, burned–

"Hell and damnation, girl! Put it out!"

A heavy grip slammed into her shoulder, squeezed and twisted. The pain snapped through Anna, and she gritted her teeth and fought down the energy scalding her limbs. It took her long seconds to restrain it, lying there on the rough floor, the heat dwindling until it was nothing but faint warmth beneath her skin.

She pulled her hands up, looking for burns, but all the flames had left were scorched sleeves. The screaming voices sank back into a muted whisper. Ashes painted her smooth fingers. "I don't . . . " she started, then her voice failed her. "I don't under–"

"Huldah-taught for sure," a voice called, and a scatter of laughter answered.

"Like she just took her first gulp of shine," Kezia said. She loomed overhead, her hand fastened at the base of Anna's neck, and her grip clenched a fraction, enough to make Anna hiss out a breath. Then she let go, rubbing her forearms. "Just sneaks up on you, handling that much power. Burns you up, makes you spit over yourself like a baby. You had your taste, now, so get your breath back. Try not to set us all ablaze."

Anna hauled herself up, wooden leg dragging awkwardly, her cheeks burning in a confusing rush of fear and shame. She limped around the pew and sat, shaken, pulling her legs up off of the floor. Around her the chatter of the little crowd rose again, sly and amused.

She waited for the headache, for the world to spin out from under her, for the wave of exhaustion to crash against her body. Yet she felt nothing of the kind; the pulsing in her head was different, frustrated almost, as if something prowling inside her was scratching to be let out. Needles of energy wound deliriously under her skin. Her mind felt cold and keen as a razor blade.

She rubbed the bridge of her nose with warm fingers, trying to make sense of it, and barely noticed the sound of soft footsteps on the boards. The bench wobbled as the young woman in the short dress sat beside her, bare toes touching the floor.

"Anna, right?"

Too late now to say nothing. "That's right."

Mary scooted a bit closer, looking straight ahead. When she spoke her voice was quiet, directed to nobody in particular. "You got no clue what happens here at all."

"Sure I do," Anna said.

"You think you got them fooled?" The woman's dark brown hair had a chewed look about the tips, and as she spoke she twisted the fabric of her ragged cotton dress. "They ain't fooled. They don't pay attention, is all. Too busy watching each other. But I was watching you. I saw you staring at the skulls, and I saw the look on your face when the fire came out your fingers. You didn't mean for that, did you?"

Anna's knuckles tightened on the bench. "You saying something?"

Now the young woman did look at her, and her brown eyes caught Anna's and held them. She leaned in, the scent of whiskey on her lips. "I'm saying… I'm warning you."

"Warning me?"

"You ain't much of a witch, are you? No, don't get mad. I ain't either. Never was much of anything, till I came to be mixed up in all this. Wanted to be, sure. Was quick enough attending, soon as the stranger came knocking at my window. And once you start coming… once it knows your name… " Mary chewed her lip. "But you. You got here 'cause of Huldah, so it don't know you. It didn't pick you."

"What didn't pick me?"

"Huldah didn't tell you anything about us, did she? Thought not." Mary's gaze flicked away, settled back. "Well, let me tell you something, Anna. I don't mind stealing milk, or laying husbands that ain't mine, or even snatching a little breath to tide me over. That's all I wanted. But they wanted more, and now they're slithering in the wind and swapping skins, all drunk on stolen souls, and they don't have much time for them with simpler tastes–"

"You can't steal souls," Anna said, working to keep her voice steady. But she was thinking of the whispering that hummed in her ears, just past the threshold of hearing. She was thinking about the screams. "There's none alive can do that."

"We couldn't," Mary said. "But *it* could. And it taught us how."

Anna opened her mouth, stopped, and closed it again. "Why tell me?"

"I had to." A flicker of uncertainty crossed Mary's face. "I saw you. You felt it, didn't you? You feel it now, all the way in your bones. Maybe you like having all that power. But I saw your face when the fire came. You were scared. And if that scares you, then you don't want to be here when the Raven Mocker comes."

Outside the empty black windows the wind picked up, whistling through the cracks in the walls. Curlicues of flame licked at the chill air. In their huddles on the pews, the other witches' heads tilted up toward the sky.

"That's them," Mary said in her flat voice. Her cold hand touched Anna O'Brien's. "Hollow Jenny and the rest. Stay quiet. You don't want to be mixed up in this."

She rose from the pew and padded away on soft bare feet, and did not look back.

Gusts whipped outside, howling against shattered roof and the ruined steeple. Black shadows flared and slithered along the piled wood, nesting in the empty sockets of the raven skulls. Clouds rolled over the distant stars.

"They're here!" Kezia called. She swept a hand up, pointing into the swirling sky. High against the moonlit clouds appeared a scatter of distant specks, flying toward them on the gale. They grew with terrible speed, tumbling like dead leaves on the air, ragged bolts of cloth twisting serpentine patterns in the crosswinds. The skies echoed with harsh laughter.

Anna stared at the altar, listening to the cacophony swell outside. It had been a week of careful preparation and planning before she'd confronted Huldah Jurgens, and even then she'd barely escaped. Huldah had been one hag, alone and half-savage in the backwoods; soon the ruined church would be swarming with dozens of them. Forget not drawing attention. She had to go, now, break for the door and sprint for the safety of the trees and lose herself in the cold and the dead leaves and the cliffs–

Her mouth took on a bitter twist at the thought. Run? Her running days were over. She wouldn't make it out of the church yard before they caught her. Nothing to do but sit, stiff and still, hands gripping her knees. Nothing to do but watch the hags come.

They poured in through the gaping holes in the ceiling, a ragged flood of yellow eyes and matted hair, the air alive with shrieking noise. Some skittered upside down along the rotting roof timbers, winding sideways down the beams until they reached the floor. Others hung like bats on the walls, tatters flapping in the breeze. They huddled in gnarled heaps on the pews, clung to the roof with bony fists, too many to count. Dirty bodies pressed so closely against Anna that her skin crawled under her coat.

"Jenny!" voices called from the crowd. "Hollow Jenny! Speak!"

A spindly figure rose from the crowd nearest to the fire, balancing on long, twisted legs. Spiderweb wrinkles spread over her naked body, sagging skin pooling loosely around her joints. Harsh green eyes glared out of a crooked face. She raised her skeletal hands high, wrists contorting in circular patterns, long nails translucent in the light. "Sisters!"

Silence fell among the throng. The hag's head turned slowly, her gaze sweeping the crowd. Anna started to look down, but too late. Their eyes met.

For a long moment the hag's eye bore down on her. Anna stared back, face blank. Her heart pounded in her ears. Then, just as suddenly as it had locked with hers, the gaze moved on.

Anna realized she'd been holding her breath and carefully let it out. So that was Hollow Jenny: a gnarled thing standing before a sea of empty faces, its face the emptiest of all.

"Oh, sisters." Hollow Jenny's jawbone cracked and popped beneath her skin as she spoke. "Brothers. Have you *heard* the news?"

"Tell us," came the answering hiss. "Tell us!"

"I dreamt," Jenny said. The words squirmed like maggots in her black teeth. "I dreamt hard days coming. I dreamt stars falling like corn kernels, I dreamt the moon dwindling like melting ice. I dreamt an empty night spreading across the skies, and I saw the thing that made it so. You know its name?"

"*Kalona Ayeliski,*" murmured the crowd. The fire flicked.

"I have become so much! I was weak once, sisters, weak as them that go tilling in the soil, weak as them that scrabble for bread. No more. Once fear of others held me back. Little rats clung to me, holding me down with little wants and needs. Little lives! But I traded that skin. I traded my weakness! Now I am strong, and I know the name of the thing that made it so."

"*Kalona Ayeliski.*" The voices swelled. Darkness rippled outside the windows.

"That great witch-thing, hated by the savages and their 'medicine men!' But we know better, don't we? We know that town beneath the mountain, empty rooms and white bones, and what lead us down to drink it dry. We know the ghosts we wove into the walls, their wails and cries, and their sweet taste on our lips. Boards grown fat with stolen souls! The lowest hag lifted and changing her skin! I dreamed that! And I saw the return of the thing that made it so!"

The witches roared. "*Kalona Ayeliski!*"

"The month turns!" howled Hollow Jenny. Her wrists twisted toward the sky, boneless beneath the wrinkled skin. "Midnight comes, and with it the *Kalona Ayeliski*, the Stranger Come Knocking, the Thief of Years! The Raven Mocker comes tonight!"

The congregation roared. Fists shook in the air over wild faces, eyes glowing in ecstacy. Figures leapt up and began to dance, fingers clicking and teeth gnashing in a hellish storm of sound. The warped walls shook, flurries of dust tumbling in the air. The skulls on the altar rattled under the stamp of feet.

"And what have we brought it?" Jenny screamed over the tumult. "What have you done this month past, brothers and sisters? You! Tell us!"

A wizened thing leapt from his perch on the wall. "I swore to a girl her tinker-man would be forever hers! I tempted the him to his death with flickering lights, and sucked his dying soul out of his body. Then I boiled his bones for witchballs and scattered them about his love's house. Sickened her! Killed her!" He drew forth a dirty jar from the folds of his cloak and held it up. "Here are their souls, twisted together forever. Am I not just?"

There were approving shrieks from the huddled masses. The flames blazed before the altar.

"Another!" howled Jenny. "What of you? What have you done this month past?"

Kezia heaved herself up, drawing her broad shoulders back as she faced the crowd. "I heard a newborn crying and crept through its keyhole. I kissed it a dozen times or two, till its skin got pale and its crying got soft. Then I drew out its breath and stole its soul, and left it there for its parents to find. I gifted them nine more months of quiet." She spread her hands, her eyes swallowed by the pleasant wrinkles of her smile. "Am I not kind?"

Harsh laughter echoed through the ruins, and crooked hands beat against withered thighs. Another leapt up to speak, and another, a growing litany of cruelty and murder, hexings and hag-ridings, and all of them ending with stolen souls. Anna's smile was a rictus against her face. She felt sick holding it there, sick for smiling. What would she do if Jenny called on her? What would she say?

"What have you done, Mary dear? What have you done this month past?"

Mary stood slowly. "I withered the field of a man who vexed me," she said. "I soured his milk in the pail and stole some for myself."

"That's all?" cried a hag hanging from the roof timbers.

"That's *all*?" Jenny's lip curled. "Where are the souls you promised to bring? Where is the misery you swore to make?"

Mary's voice sharpened. "I put him in his place. Now he keeps me happy. Gives me first pick of all he grows and more."

Sharp faces peeked over Mary's shoulder. "Oh, he keeps you happy, does he?"

"Grows things for you? Plants seeds for you?"

A vein pulsed at Mary's neck. "That's enough for me, sisters."

"But that's not enough for us," hissed Jenny. "Is this what you traded yourself for? The petty torment of cattle? Crops? Kisses? Never want to bring your share, do you? Never want to pull your weight? That's not enough for it, and it's not enough for us, you waste of a thing—"

Mary rocked backward as if she'd been struck. "I didn't trade myself for you!" she spat. "I'm not yours to tell off! You stand up there playing preacher if you like, but I'm not yours! What've I seen for my time here? Cold nights in a church, screaming in my head when I conjure, headaches and shakes from holding it in?" She slapped the bench, the brittle wood cracking under her palm. "A fine trade I made!"

Jenny's eyes gleamed. "And you reject the gift?"

The crowd rustled. Anna glimpsed Kezia standing back, heavy arms folded, her face hard.

"I brew and hex, Jenny. I can't fly." Mary stepped back, her fingers squeezing the rough cotton of her dress. Around her, a few of the other witches edged away. She paused, looking at the eyes focused on her, and her face grew ugly with fear. "I don't *want* to fly. I don't want to crawl out of my skin. I wanted to live as I liked. Not this."

"It gave you power," Jenny said softly. A small smile tugged at her cheeks. She rose from her crouch on the pew, wrinkled body unfolding. The others pressed closer, their eyes hungry.

"Just let me go." Mary took another step backward. "Let me go, Jenny. You don't want me here. You never wanted me here. Just let me go—"

Jenny's smile stretched over her face, bunching in folds of meat down her neck, spreading in ripples down her body. Something stirred and twisted under her skin. "Weak," she said. Her lips drew back from black teeth, then further, and further yet. The flesh underneath was wet and red.

Mary's nerve broke. She bolted for the door, but with a great shriek a pack of hags flowed over her. Hands snatched at her arms, her shoulders, ripping at her cotton dress. She lashed out, snarling, kicking, but the crush of bodies bore her down. A spatter of hot blood splashed on the floorboards.

Anna stood rooted to the spot, horrified gaze fixed on Jenny's shaking form. Flesh ripped and flapped around bony feet. Long fingers curled and stretched in the cold air.

"No!" Mary shrieked, her eyes fixed on the unfolding thing pulling itself out of Jenny's skin. "Goddamn you! No!"

The flesh fell away. With an inhuman screech the thing whirled off the pew and slammed into Mary, jaws unhinging to latch down over her face. It pressed itself on her chest, bony fingers clawing at her wrists, teeth digging into her cheeks. The sticky bands of its throat began to gulp in slow, rhythmic waves.

Mary thrashed, her eyes wide with terror. Even from across the church, even with the rotting mouth pressed against her lips, her scream went on and on, the sound cracking as if the voice was being torn from her lungs. It was an inhuman sound. Anna shoved forward against the crowd without thinking, her fingers clenching into fists, but a hand planted itself on her chest and held her back.

"Don't," hissed the nearest hag. "Let Jenny have her fun. You'll drink with the rest of us when she's through."

The thrashing in Mary's limbs loosened, her voice giving way at last, leaving only choking, agonized whimpers. The thing ground itself on her shaking body, throat sucking, green eyes staring out of black sockets. Her pale legs flopped in boneless spasms. Flesh bunched around the thing's bony fingers like a sheet.

Rasping breaths. Brown eyes rolled up in Mary's slack face, dwindled, and disappeared. Her skin sagged in an empty shrivel on the floor.

Joints popped wetly as the thing shifted. It dug its hands into the limp mouth and with a rheumatic hiss pulled itself inside. The flesh jerked, lumps and folds roiling across its surface. Bones snapped, cracked, reformed. Then the body sat up, adjusting the dress where it had slipped off her shoulders.

"I've wanted to do that for *months*," said the thing with Mary's voice. Green eyes stared out from her lids. She rose and padded back up the church, bones bulging and sliding under her skin. Boards creaked under her feet. The crowd parted for her as she leapt up onto the edge of a pew, balancing on her toes; her hands slid up and down the curves of her new body, worming inside the cotton dress. "Aren't I pretty again, sisters?"

"Show us!" howled the crowd. "Show us!"

Jenny grinned. Her arm swept out in a sudden arc, the dress snapping and tearing in a trail of dirty fabric. The congregation screamed as it landed in the fire and she stood bare before them. "Look! Isn't this a fine skin for Hollow Jenny? Her power is mine, and her body is mine, and the years of her life are mine too!"

"*All* her power?" called Kezia.

"Don't be greedy, Jenny," whined a short hag perched on a broken stool. "Share her, Jenny. Share."

Jenny tossed Mary's hair. Rolling back on her heels, she opened her mouth and exhaled. Something white and indistinct fluttered weakly into the air. "Take her!"

A hag leapt up and snatched at the fluttering object with long, ragged nails. It tumbled toward a pew, then veered away toward another, its movements panicked. Another arm snapped up, and another. Then a hand closed over the wispy thing and pulled it down. It resisted, twisting away with surprising strength, but the witch only laughed and forced it into the wooden wall.

Static snapped across the floor. The congregation groaned in ecstasy, harsh light dripping from their mouths. Power leapt along Anna's limbs, roiled under her skin, bled out of her eyes. Her feet lost contact with the floor, the world tilting as she was born aloft on a surging tide of energy. The screams pulsed in her ears, faint. One of them she knew.

Twisted shapes scrambled wildly through the air, rags flapping like lazy wings. Anna's gorge pressed against her lips, burned her tongue. She flailed her leg out and hooked it under the lip of the bench, hauling herself back down. Seizing hold of the pew in front of her, she gulped in a breath, fighting down the urge to vomit. Not now. She couldn't lose her stomach now, they'd see—

"Witch soul," breathed the woman closest, her eye rolling in its socket.

"She made herself useful in the end," cried another lolling from the rafters, and laughter scraped the air. "Oh, the taste of her! The larder's growing tonight. Let's put the others in!"

"Not yet!" Jenny said. "We've more to hear, don't we? More praise to give!"

The throng sunk back to their seats, movements drunken, crawling up the walls and settling on the tops of the pews. Another witch stood, spoke. Anna's hands clamped the bench. Noise washed around her, vague and drowned out by the hammer of her heartbeat. Panic clawed at her gut, and she nearly stood, nearly ran, nearly brought a fist down on the witch in front of her, nearly called up flame, nearly–

She shut her eyes and gritted her teeth, a fierce ache creeping along her jaw. She'd give herself away if she tried to keep quiet. The horror would show on her face, the turmoil inside her would burst its banks, and then they'd swarm over her, pin her, overwhelm her. Leave her as empty as houses down at the crossroads, empty as Jenny's skin on the floor. She shoved that thought away. There had to be some way out, didn't there? If she couldn't run, and couldn't keep quiet, than she'd have to talk. But what was there to say?

Think. What had she seen? Firelight on the terrible altar. The stamp and snap of withered limbs. Ugly fear rising in Mary's eyes, and touching the eyes of those around her. Jenny's mouth twisting in greed, the look blossoming across the congregation. Fear and greed, and the shadows on the raven skulls—

The room snapped back into focus. Anna drew a deep breath and stood. "I got something to say!"

Jenny rolled a smooth hand in her direction. "And what have you brought for us?"

"A question," Anna said. Her heart hammered. "I'm newly come here. Who's the Raven Mocker? Why's it helping us?"

Laughter rippled over the broken pews. Jenny preened before the crowd. "Newly come here? Well, rejoice! When the savages ran among the hills, the *Kalona Ayeliski* took from sickbeds, crept into the houses of the old, took their last years for itself. It was weak then. But now it has made itself strong, vast and powerful as the black between stars! And it has called us here, led us, shared its power with us. It has given us so much—"

"Everything but common sense." Anna said, her voice loud, hardly shaking at all. "I mean, I seen some fools in my day. But I never seen anyone worship a thing that means to kill them."

The congregation went deathly silent. Outside the wind buffeted the steeple tower, lapping chill and sharp beneath the scudding clouds. Rafters groaned softly under shifting weight. Heads swivelled toward Anna, expressions' intent, a court of owls regarding an impudent mouse.

"What's that?" The closest hag snaked forward, words clipped and tight. "What do you mean?"

"Can't you see it?" Anna said. "I mean—"

Jenny landed on a nearby pew, the bench buckling under the impact, splinters raining onto the floor. Figures ducked away from her, hissing in complaint. "That's enough. Who are you, little witch?"

"That's Anna," Kezia said, crossing her arms. "A wanderer."

"Anna." Hollow Jenny's black tongue darted out and licked her lips. Mary's lips. "You're new to me. New to us, and too new to be saying such things. Sit down."

"I'm warning you. Don't you want them to hear it?"

A murmuring started up, a chorus of muffled whispers and sidelong glances. "What warning?" said a scarred hag on a nearby bench.

Jenny's lips crept back from her teeth. "There's nothing to hear! You're nobody, and you know nothing. Be quiet."

"Break her, Hollow Jenny!" hissed the pale hag on the stool. "I like her skin!"

But the muttering was spreading, more voices rising in the gloom. Pews creaked and scraped across the floorboards. Heads rose above the sitting figures, craning for a better look. The scarred hag stood. "I'll hear her," she said. "You got a warning?"

"Sisters! She's just a—"

"You speak for them, Jenny?" Anna said. "All of them?"

Jenny's mouth worked. Her green eyes fixed on Anna's throat. "I—"

"Oh, let her talk," Kezia said, and her eyes glittered as she looked at Jenny. "What's the harm? We can always share her after."

Anna's heart thudded in her chest, but she crossed her eyes and stared. Hollow Jenny's gaze raked Kezia's face, sharp and suspicious. She cut a quick glance at the muttering crowd, and Anna saw her weighing it, thinking it over. The green eyes bore into her. Finally the hag sank back onto her haunches and gave a tight nod.

"Friends," Anna said. The word tasted dirty in her mouth, but she spat it out and went on. A sea of faces stared at her, hard and gnarled as old wood. "I got no fancy words, like Jenny does. But here's what I see. The Raven Mocker came knocking at your shutters, told you it'd teach you how to steal souls. Taught you to steal and hoard them all in one place, and set you to bringing in more all the time—"

"It set us to nothing!" Jenny said. "We hold in common, all in common, even the *Kalona Ayeliski*—"

"Let her speak!"

"Why'd it do it?" Anna said over the rising clamor. "Tell me that! This Raven Mocker can take its own souls. It knows the way of it. What does it want? Your altar? Your praise? I'm asking! Why does the Raven Mocker need us?"

Jenny's mouth gaped. "Wickedness," she said. "Spiteful wickedness!"

But the hags shifted, tongues darting out to touch their lips. Some had turned in their seats to stare at the altar, watching the light slither across the tangled logs and polished bone. Anna was teetering now, balancing precariously on the crest of their attention, and she could see by the look in Hollow Jenny's eyes what would happen if she fell.

"Don't play coy," yipped a hag on the wall. "Don't toy with your hair! What are you saying?"

Anna spun to face her. "You have your animals over for supper? Set a plate for them? It's *farming* us! It teaches us to hoard its food, inside the church, inside us, and it waits. Like we're cattle left out in the woods, fattening ourselves for a feast. What happens when we're fat enough? What then?"

"The Raven Mocker's been good to us!" Jenny hissed.

"I been good to people!" Anna shot back. "I been good to lots of folk. Even as I spoiled their milk and sickened their wives and rotted their crops. I took what I wanted from them, and none was ever better to them than me! Who wears her cruelty on her face?"

Thoughtful expressions regarded her in the gloom, cracked nails scratching at shrunken chins, breath hissing through crooked teeth. Others were looking at Jenny with intent, hungry expressions. A flash of uncertainty crossed the hag's face.

Anna saw it and pushed harder. "All the bodies and souls you've stolen, you think it can't happen to you? You think you're special?"

Kezia's cut in over Jenny's croak of rage. "A worrying tale, it's true. But what, then? You want us to flee?"

"We could," Anna said. "But we're strong now, sisters. Why should it be the Raven Mocker who gets fat off us? Think of the power Mary's soul put into the walls, and she was just a sad little thing. If we kill it—"

There was an eruption of noise at that. Voices hissed and croaked over each other, hands waving, fingers pointing at her, at each other, at the altar. Arguments broke out in the corners. The flames beat angrily at the cold air.

"You don't know what you're asking," sneered a crone. "No witch can kill the Raven Mocker!"

"Only a righteous gaze harms the *Kalona Ayeliski*," Jenny snarled. "Only a righteous power, looking it in its face. It does not show its true face, little witch. It laughs at shot and conjure. It laughs at iron!"

"It comes here masked?" Anna snapped back, fast. "Here? Who's righteous here? What's it afraid of?"

"You can't kill it!" Jenny's voice was ragged. "Why would we even try? Sisters—"

"Imagine it," said the scarred hag. Fear and greed fought across her face. "Imagine if we could. With power like that I'd never walk the ground again."

"You're mad," Jenny screamed, whirling on her. "Mad as old Huldah. Mad as this snip of a girl! It's nearly midnight! All of you, sit down—"

Shouting boiled on the air. Moving fast, Anna reached under the pew and pulled out her bag and walking stick. She turned for the door, unnoticed in the tumult, her heart racing in her chest. Time was slowing around her, thick as molasses, but she pushed through, step by step, the din rising around her. Ghostly whispers grew as she approached the doorway. She was going to make it. She reached out toward the latch.

There was a rush of air and a thunderous crack. Jenny's palm slammed against the door in front of Anna's face, striking the wood so hard that the flesh on the back of her hand split to reveal the pale wet meat quivering underneath.

"You go nowhere," growled the hag. Fetid breath washed along the back of Anna's neck. Her voice dropped, became almost sweet. "You want us to kill the *Kalona Ayeliski*? Why are you sneaking away? Do I have to drag you back, wise little witch? Shall I find someone braver for your skin?"

Anna's hand squeezed tight on her walking stick. All she could see was the heavy wood smashing itself to splinters across the black teeth, but she took a deep breath and turned, her face inches from Jenny's. She opened her mouth—

Something knocked at the door.

Silence stretched across the ruined church. The squabbling congregation froze, sitting still in their perches, hanging white-knuckled on the walls. Jenny paced back, bare feet sliding on the boards, eyes wide. Anna moved as well, her leg stiff, hand back to guide her way to the wall. Above them the moon hung, still and perfect in the middle of the sky.

There came a strange groaning, the sound of heavy wood dragging itself slowly, fitfully, across the pitted stone. The door shuddered slowly open, and beyond rolled the long, empty slopes of the bald. Deep cold bled through the open doorway, freezing Anna's bones with its touch. The flames dwindled before the altar, red tongues shriveling and drawing back, pulling the shadows in from where they hid among the bones.

The hags' eyes glowed in the dark. "It's come," muttered voices. "It's come. *Kalona Ayeliski!* The Stranger Come Knocking!"

The air pressed against Anna's face, digging at her skin, dragging at her limbs. The world outside spun and grew taut, stretching out into an endless corridor, and at the farthest end walked a hunched figure. Slow steps carried it swiftly across the landscape, blurring forward with uncanny motion, a ragged cloak flapping behind. Its movements echoed with a deep, horrible wrongness, out of sync with itself, a cut-out thing dancing across a painted background.

"Who is precious to me, little hags?" The voice echoed far away and whispered in her ear, metallic and raspy, the syllables strange and swallowed. "Who is precious to me?"

Anna pressed herself against the wall, her eyes watering, the pressure building in her skull. The weight of footsteps crushed her chest, a hollow, steady pounding, heavier and heavier as the ragged thing approached. She squeezed her eyes shut, afterimages dancing in the dark, trying to block out the thing flying across the warped landscape toward them. The despair she'd fought all night threatened to overwhelm her.

The wall hummed under her fingers, the power of those stolen lives stirring inside her, pacing to get out. Would she draw on them, if it came to it? To save her own life? Would it even be enough? Nothing she could do to set them free, nothing, short of tearing the wall down board by board–

The pressure against her face fell away. She opened her eyes.

The Raven Mocker stood in the doorway. Its tattered cloak fell like folded wings down its shoulders, pooling on the stones in a mess of snaking threads. A wooden mask hung over its head, crude and stained,

shaped like a raven's skull. A strange and bitter chill bled from the empty eye sockets.

Jenny's fingers dug at the air, her face slack against her skull. The crowd stared.

"It is time, little hags," said the Raven Mocker. Its voice dragged painfully against Anna's ears. Jerking steps carried it past her, cloak hissing on the floor. Those in its path scrambled away, their motions abrupt and strange against the stillness of the crowd. The Raven Mocker's head swung to track them, the mask silhouetted against the dull glow of the coals. Just as quickly it swung back, head cocked, taking in the silent surroundings. "Is this my welcome?"

Anna again had the sense of teetering on the brink, a chasm on either side, the wind snatching at her feet. It felt like the whole congregation was holding its breath.

"Great *Kalona Ayeliski,*" Jenny said, her voice rough. "We—"

"You hungry?" Kezia said. Around her, eyes narrowed in the gloom.

"I come." The Raven Mocker loomed over them. The tatters of its cloak lifted lazily in the air. "I come, and you will feed me. I hunger, little hags."

Kezia heaved herself up. "So do we," she said, and leapt.

It all hung in the air for a second; the harsh flames blossoming from Kezia's curled fingers, the Raven Mocker's mask swinging up, rags and tatters flaring in the air. Jenny's gaping mouth. Kezia's hand snapped down in a white-hot flash. The Raven Mocker staggered.

"Now, sisters!" Anna screamed. Horrified faces turned to look at her. "Now! Like we agreed!"

"Agreed?" The Raven Mocker shot forward, a black column in the air, the mask snapping out. Kezia's body spun away, breaking against the wall with a crack of snapping bone. She tumbled down limply in a shower of splinters and fell face up, the head a twisted wreck, limbs twitching. The Raven Mocker turned to look at them. "*Agreed*, little hags? You *dare*—"

The congregation exploded into motion. Hags scrambled for the roof, hissing in terror. Others whirled across the warped floors, bitter light erupting from their hands and feet, plummeted from the rafters in showers of dust. Bodies slammed into the Raven Mocker, swarming over each other as they slapped and snatched at the wooden mask. Snarling lips flipping back to reveal jagged brown teeth.

The Raven Mocker surged beneath them. Its cloak flew upward with a sound like tearing flesh, coiling black shafts unfolding in infinite patterns until they brushed the roof. Those clinging to the fabric shrieked as it clawed its way up their forearms and pulled them in. Others were thrown clear, slamming into the walls with enough force to rattle the floor. The strands began to flap, faster and faster, melting into undulating sheets that beat the air like enormous wings. The witches' howls were drowned out by another cry, a rasping, terrible scream that knocked Anna back against the wall.

Another body hit the floor in a pulp of shattered meat. Flames guttered in its clenched hands, licking in time to the fading pulse of its blood. Scattered coals smoldered amid the pews. Anna stumbled for the door, keeping her head down, an arm over her mouth. The whispering in her ears quickened. Behind her, the rotting floorboards caught fire.

And still the hags came. They skittered through the air, leaping up the currents, swarming over the infinite flapping thing. The swarm of fighting bodies slammed back and forth across the walls, shingles exploding in a stinging hail of dust and shrapnel, the walls shaking under the repeated impacts. "The hoard!" screamed the scarred hag. Pale teeth shone through a cheek laid open. "It'll break the hoard! Help us!"

Anna ducked a tumble of falling rubble. Flickers of red light ate at the floor, smoke pulsing up in a choking haze. "Smash the mask!"

The Raven Mocker heard. It turned on Anna and shot forward, the smoke parting around it. But the scarred hag was already twisting in the air. Her arm arced out and a sheet of bitter light collided with the wooden mask, knocking it askew. For the barest of seconds, the Raven Mocker's face stood revealed.

Anna's heart stopped. A kaleidoscope spun across her vision. Flies crawled under her skin. Maggots wormed through her bones. Rot sprouted along her tongue, and she could taste it pouring along her throat, hear her flesh peeling, feel her stomach swell–

The spirit shrieked as if scalded, ducking away. The wooden mask slipped back into place; the Raven Mocker's beak snapped out and speared the scarred hag, hammering her into a red ruin on the floorboards. Flesh sizzled and smoked in the air.

Anna sucked in air and retched. There was an iron taste in her mouth, and she realized dimly that she'd bitten her tongue. She struggled weakly up off the floor, ears buzzing, unsteady, her eyes seared and hurting. Around her the church was a sickening whirl of bodies and smoke and harsh light, shadows leaping and clawing along the walls. Timbers snapped and buckled in the rafters, plummeting to the ground, dragging clumps of the building with them. Flames leapt and chewed at the back of the building.

The whispering roared inside her, hungry, cutting in and out with every shattering collision. Heat rolled against her face. She leaned against the wall. What had she been doing? Confusion sucked at her, made her reel on her feet. She looked up in time to see Jenny's twisted face lunging across the snapped pews toward her, arm blurring, jaws twisting in a feral scream.

The blow knocked her through the door. She hung for a moment, air rushing against her face, and then the ground flew up and everything went white. Cold grass bit against her cheek and she wrestled herself up onto an elbow, ears ringing as she stared at the distant building. Light whirled and raged above the church, the building shuddering under repeated blows. Smoke billowed in great plumes toward the sky. She pushed herself up—

Jenny exploded out of the dark, inarticulate, snarling. Mary's skin was half seared away, and what remained flapped grotesquely against her wet bones. One murderous eye stared out of a crumpled face. In seconds the hag was on Anna, bowling her over and pinning her arms. The oozing lower body swung up to straddle her chest, knees digging into her sides.

"Your fault," Hollow Jenny hissed, words slurring through tattered lips. "All of this, your fault. So smart, weren't you? So *clever*. Turning them against me to snatch the power for yourself. Look what you've done!"

Skeletal fingers tightened on Anna's wrists. Anna thrashed, bones creaking under the implacable grip. Her feet dug helplessly at the ground.

Thunder rolled over the bald. The Raven Mocker erupted through the disintegrating church roof, flames streaming from its shoulders, ragged shapes flitting desperately around it. Hags climbed desperately for the clouds. There was a drunken wobble in the spirit's flight as it pursued them, a sickly stutter in its wings; still the wooden beak flashed out, picking bodies out of the air and snapping them in two. Screams carried on the wind.

"I'll not die," Jenny snarled into Anna's ear. Muscles gleamed wetly in the faint light of the inferno. The ravaged body ground against her, its touch sickening. The weight of it squeezed the breath from her lungs. "No, not tonight. I'll not burn in the dawn. I'll have you, Anna!"

A hand gripped Anna's chin, squeezing her mouth open. Seeping jaws cracked and shifting under the rags of Mary's face. "How does it feel, you one-legged bitch? Can't run now. Can't talk your way out of this one. All that power, and you wasted it. Look at me, little witch. Look at me—"

Anna's wooden leg slammed up, her knee driving into Hollow Jenny's raw back. The hag's mouth opened in surprise and pain, and in that second Anna jammed her freed fist into the open jaw, curling her fingers against the soft lining her throat. Jenny struggled, choking, eye rolling wildly in its socket. Jagged teeth buried themselves in Anna's arm, blood squeezing up through the ragged jacket sleeves. Wet tissue crumbled beneath Anna's fingers. For a heartbeat, Jenny's thighs lost their grip on her chest.

Breath rushed back into Anna's lungs. All the anger, all the despair, all the desperation roiled inside her, scorching hot and powered by the vengeful screaming of murdered souls. The burning rushed through up her stomach like a flood, spiraling along her bloody arm, and in the last second Anna O'Brien pulled Hollow Jenny's head close.

"There's your power," she said. "Choke on it."

The fire erupted from her closed fist. It boiled out of Jenny's skull, licking from her empty eye, burning away the skin, the muscle, everything, until the skull itself exploded in a shower of black brittle flakes and the body of Hollow Jenny fell atop her, twitching its last against the cold ground.

Anna lay there a moment, head spinning. Twisting, she worked her hands into the sticky wreckage on top of her and pushed, breath sobbing in her throat, until the carcass rolled away to flop on the grass. With faltering steps she stumbled to her feet, hair blowing free in the wind. Agony rolled in slow waves through her body.

A low groan filtered through the night, the church steeple leaning, slipping, falling in a roar of snapping rubble. Burning walls shattered beneath the weight, dust billowing into the dark. The impact rattled up Anna's wooden leg. Her ears popped; the pulse and coil of restless energy snuffed out as if it had never been. In the distance, fleeing specks plunged abruptly from the sky.

The Raven Mocker stood waiting on the slope.

Anna sighed, bending over slowly to pick up her hat with shaking fingers. The spirit's gaze bored into her back as she moved. She put the hat on her head, straightened it. Tucked the hair out of her eyes. Her bag lay some way off in the grass, and she hobbled over to it and pulled the leather strap up her shoulder. Only then did she turn.

"Well?" she said.

Dark spatters painted the beak of the wooden mask. The ragged cloak swept and tossed in wind, blacker than black. Yet there was something drained about it, diminished, a thin body swimming in a lake of tattered fabric. It shifted under her gaze, a quiver running through its body. "Who are you?"

"Nobody," Anna said. Blood oozed from her arm, curling down her fingers to spatter the grass. "Nothing."

On the slope, timbers groaned and crackled in the flames. Sparks whirled on the wind.

"You did this," the Raven Mocker said. "Turned my hags against me."

Anna stood shivering in the cold. Her leg ached. "You were going to eat them anyway, weren't you? Wasn't that your plan?"

"Eat them?" Quills flared along the Raven Mocker's cloak. "I ate them. The power faded from them even as they died. My chosen hags. My precious hags. No more sickbeds, sipping away the last years of men! I taught them to tease out whole souls, proper souls, held in common and used by all. They would take and take and take, so that their power had no end, and mine would be greater still. Beyond the dreams of man and night-goer! Now they are dead and the hoard is destroyed. Souls flit free upon the air. You did this."

"You helped," Anna said. "Couldn't have torn that church down myself."

"Tricks," the Raven Mocker hissed. "The power of the Kalona Ayeliski is greater than you could dream, little witch. I will find another church. I will begin again." It moved a quick, hopping step in her direction, limbs shifting beneath the baggy cloak. "I will begin with you."

A single crack spiraled up the surface of the moonlit mask.

"Think so?" Anna said.

The Raven Mocker hopped closer, neck coiled back like a bird preparing to strike. Then it stopped. Hair-thin fissures sprouted up and down the wood, spreading slowly over the carved beak. It shrank back. "What is happening?"

"Your mask slipped." Anna said. "Didn't you feel it? Only a righteous power hurts the *Kalona Ayeliski,* if they see it's true face—"

"You?" The Raven Mocker's voice was a rough cry.

"Me," Anna said. "Why not?"

"You lie," the Raven Mocker said softly. "I see the power rolling in you. You are a hag. You traded yourself like the rest—"

Anna's grey eyes flashed under her hat. "You don't know what I traded, or why. I saw you under that mask, Raven Mocker, and you're nothing special. Just an old crow, picking over old bones. I've seen my fill of you." She made a fist, skinned knuckles aching, and for a moment her hand glowed, coal-red beneath her skin. "You want to know who I am? Come on then. You can even go first."

Moonlight shone on the quaking grass.

A piece of wood flaked away from the Raven Mocker's beak, then another. Scraps of cloth whirled away in the wind. Its eyes flickered. With a grinding shriek it jerked upwards into the air, its cloak stretching threadbare and worn against the stars. The world blurred with the sound of beating wings, the night sky rippling like water. Then it was gone. On the ground, a pair of black feathers crumbled into dust on the breeze.

Anna's leg gave. The glow in her fist went out. She fell awkwardly to her knees, stomach wriggling like a snake. Even as her hands met the grass she was vomiting, convulsions rolling up her gut, the sick burning her throat. Her hands shook on the grass. Exhaustion swept over her with the weight of a landslide, battering down the last of her defenses, and it all flowed up; empty houses, blood on the church boards, Mary's screaming face, the rags of it slapping against Jenny's skull. The wooden mask darting toward her through the smoke. How close had she come? How close?

But she was alive. She spat and sank back, breathing harsh. Lifting hands sticky with grime and drying blood, she rolled her sleeve up to survey the damage to her forearm, wincing at what she saw. Digging inside her satchel, she pulled out a length of rag and a poultice of yellowroot, setting them on the ground before her. With a series of pained grunts she wound both around the mangled flesh, before taking the rag's edge in her teeth and pulling it taut.

Bracken rustled in undulating waves below the cold stars. Timbers crunched and fell in the smoldering church, spitting showers of embers into the sky. Slowly, every movement strained, Anna limped over toward the fire. The heat pressing against her like a wall. She collapsed in the grass a comfortable distance away, tucking her arms inside her battered jacket. Something brushed against her face, spiderweb soft.

"Oh," she said. She pulled her legs up to her chest, wincing at the pain. "*Now* you come back?"

The black dog stepped smoothly from the shadows beside her, long legs and tangled black fur taking shape from the dark. Anna watched it lope into the burning building, nose down, sniffing the smoking rubble. Heavy jaws snapped at the air, shaking unseen things like rabbits and wolfing them down. With every bite it grew, eyes glowing, until it loomed above the timbers on legs like tree trunks. Its short ears blocked the stars.

Anna saw it then. A horde of souls bound up in the walls of a decrepit church, guarded by hags and something worse, calling out like food locked in a larder. And the black dog circling round and round, watching.

Bringing someone who could break down the door and scatter the souls to the wind. Someone who would finally let it feast.

She spat out a mouthful of blood. "Hey!"

The black dog turned to stare at her, eyes shining like distant moons. Faint starlight glittered through its coat. Tangled fur hung motionless in the wind.

"You owe me," Anna said. Her voice was raw. "My night's been hell because of you."

The dog's head tilted. Its form spun and blurred, weaving itself into the night. Its eyes lingered, pale blue and glowing against the stars, and winked out.

"Damn dog," Anna muttered. Even with the heat from the fire, a chill settled over her back, the bitter cold freezing its way through her sweaty clothes. Numbness inched its slow way up her fingers.

Her breath clouded the sharp air as she sighed. Slowly, she stretched out her unbandaged hand and closed her eyes. The cold scratched her lungs as she inhaled. Her hand twisted as she concentrated, and she felt the warm tingle gather in her stomach. She held it there. The whispering was gone from her ears, the distant rubble silent and empty, the souls fled and devoured and gone.

Anna's eyes opened. She looked at her outstretched hand, at the dull firelight playing behind her fingers. Her fist clenched. Charred wood glowed in the rippling air. Then she shuddered and exhaled, letting the prickling feeling go.

She pressed closer to the flames. The trees swayed in the distance, black against the starlight sky. When the fire finally went out she'd head that way, down into the forests under the ridgelines. Somewhere in there she'd find a place out of the wind, where the dead leaves were thick on the ground, and the cold didn't bite.

Not flying. Not flame, either. But enough, just the same.

THE REVENANT SCORE

1902

When the first movement came under her foot it was a soft shiver, like a sleeper waking from a dream. Anna O'Brien straightened and held up the lamp, the light playing over the gravestones and dried dogsbane, sparkling off the rocks. As she shifted something knocked, deep down below.

The graveyard was a small place tucked away off the logging road, in a valley five miles from the nearest home and fifteen from the nearest town. It sat in a stretch of deep soil up the logged-out slope, surrounded by folded shelves of granite. The timber company had been and gone, leaving ranks of stumps stretching away in the brittle earth, parched ground eroding out from under their roots. Only a scattered fringe of trees lingered atop the rock shelves, left by the local woodcutters out of respect for the dead. Twenty gravestones poking out of a shaded carpet of dogsbane. That was all.

It was the dead that had brought her to that quiet place, sheltered from the valley's echoes. Passing through to the north she heard a story of a rumbling grave, of a glimpse of something flitting by the timber-men, pale and faint in the moonlight. There was no pressing reason for her to go; few came up into the valley after the cut, and fewer visited the graves. But Anna took her tasks where she could find them. Besides, the lonely places suited her.

She crouched now at the base of the rock, pulling her coat tighter around her, her satchel and walking stick down at her side. The last glow was slipping over the ridgelines, the peaks darkening to black against the purple dusk. A cool breeze rustled the carpet of dried weeds. Headstones tilted in the dim glow, their names weathered, covered in dried moss and splashes of pale lichen.

"Come on," she said under her breath. "Let's see you."

The knocking came again, louder, like knuckles on a wooden lid. Shards of shattered stone bounced up from the tangle, pattering on the matted stems. A shape flickered out in the gloom, drifting up from a half-snapped headstone; white eyes huge and staring, a stomach and wrists bound in heavy links that strained against the dirt. Pale flesh rippled in the dark.

Gold, whispered a voice on the breeze. *The gold…*

Anna's hand was already slipping into her bag, feeling for her salt pouch. But she paused at the sound, the words faint and almost beyond hearing. "Gold?"

They buried it among the dead. The words spidered in her ear. *They told the dead to keep it. I am bound, laid here for the gold…until they come to claim it, any of the family left living.*

"They're cleared out," Anna said. "Whoever they are. Sold out and moved, got the homeplace broken up. Nobody's going to…"

She drifted to a halt, looking at the grave. Gold, lost and forgotten out on a timber tract, gold nobody knew was missing. What could you do with gold like that? A fine house, all furnished, a plot to call her own? But that was a thought that led her near the lip of the old despair, and she shoved it away. If there was gold, let there be gold; it wasn't hers.

I am bound, laid here for the gold…until they come to claim it, any of the family left living. The voice sighed on, low, at the edge of hearing. *Birthright gold. A coffin of gold. Who are you?*

"The one who's gonna settle you." Setting the lantern down on the ground to give herself light to work by, Anna stood, pouch in hand. She stepped toward the grave.

WRONG ONE.

The ghost jerked in the air. Something smashed into Anna like a train, knocking her backward and away, the salt spinning away into the dogsbane. She crashed into a sapling and rolled over, wheezing. Lay there a moment and pushed herself up, movements jerky, face grim. "Fine," she said, inhaling. "I'll just—"

WRONG ONE.

The thing jerked and lunged like a fish on a line, bonds cutting tight into its limbs, flesh stretching, jaws lengthening. A hard blow hammered into her back, smacking her flat into the weeds and knocking the wind out of her. Twice more Anna tried to rise and snatch in a breath, to shove the thing away, banish it; twice more she was thrown back and down, bounced against the hard-packed dirt. Finally she gave up and lay still, the ghost's voice howling overhead.

WRONG ONE. WRONG ONE. WRONG ONE.

"Fine! Alright!" She grit her teeth, thinking hard. The ghosts she'd met before were wisps, shadows, dispersed in a whisper of breath. But this was something else. Salt would handle it, she was sure, but the salt pouch was somewhere down in the weeds. It might as well be in Virginia. Some ghostbreaker.

She pushed herself back along the ground, moving slow. When her foot touched the edge of the rock shelf she went up on hands and knees, wincing. "Alright," she said. "What do you want?"

The thing hung in the air before her, skin maggot white. Black fluid wept where the bonds cut into its limbs; the links glistened, sagging in loops out of an open hole in its body, knotting around its arms. Not chains.

I am the gold, whispered the voice. *They buried it among the dead, and told the dead to keep it. I am bound, laid here for the gold…until they come to claim it, any yet living. Tell them.*

"Who on earth am I supposed to tell?"

The dogsbane shivered, unwinding, a slab of weathered stone surfacing in the lamplight. It rolled toward her and fell flat, showing her a faint name. Anna looked down at it a moment, shook her head and hauled herself up to her feet. Never walk away, she reminded herself.

"Fine. I ask around, find whoever's left from this...Herriman family? Bring them up here. You'll go then?"

Tell them.

The night stretched away over the graveyard, empty. Crickets chirped in the weeds. She lingered there a moment, waiting for a reply. Then, aching, she sighed and picked up her things, circling around the lip of the granite and heading back down the slope. Toward the road.

***

When the gunmen came into the First National Bank, Bakersmont Branch, nobody noticed. Not the tellers behind the polished wooden counter, not the businessmen waiting in line, not the guard leaning against the wall. Least of all Anna. She was focused on her reflection in the tiles, thinking over what she'd say to the teller when she got to him, and wondering if she'd be thrown out before she got the chance.

She'd walked for a day out of the clear-cut valley, heading south on a hunch, hearing on the way that some of the Herrimans had gone to live up around Bakersmont after losing the property, and that she might find a Boyce Herriman working at the bank. Anna camped in the shanties above town that night, smelling the iron smell in the air on the hillside. Three railroad lines converged at the town depot, pumping timber and mica out of the mountains and returning full of payroll cash. From above the telegraph lines spidered out over the close-crowded wood and brick buildings; down on the dirt streets, the people she passed glowed like the boom had been a reward for good behavior.

The First National Bank sat on a corner of the main street, a two-story brownstone with broad windows of glass and wrought iron. Shafts of crisp morning sunlight striped the panelled walls, glinted off the iron grating on the counter. The staff's eyes had fallen on Anna as soon as she entered the lobby, her boots squeaking on the marble tiles. Pinched faces stared from behind the counter. The guard watched her, the weight of his attention pressing down quiet and sluggish. She avoided their gaze, studying the floor.

That was why nobody paid much attention when the men came in. Not until a slight, dapper man drew a pistol and held it up, spinning it on his finger so that it caught the morning sunlight. "Down, down, down," he sang. "Lay yourselves down! This is a robbery."

Anna wheeled around in time to see a man in a cavalry hat and greatcoat tug a scarf up over his face and slip a rifle out from where he'd held it against his side. Behind him, three men pulled bandannas up over their noses. They wore their hats low. Pistols and shotguns appeared in their gloved hands.

Shrill gasps echoed against the panelling. The guard stared, open-mouthed. Abruptly he remembered himself, fumbling at his holster, and stopped when a pair of guns swiveled his way. The pistol-man's voice cracked out like a whip. "I said down!"

Anna got down. It was a slow process with her wooden leg, and she leaned on the walking stick as she went, wincing at the protest in her muscles. Then boot-leather flashed and the stick was kicked out of her hands, clattering away and dropping her hard on the marble. She arched up, eyes blazing, by instinct more than anything; the shotgun in her face stopped her cold.

"You heard the man," rumbled a deep voice above her. "Stay down."

The world narrowed, draining like a whirlpool into the the black holes of the gun barrel. Slowly, she pressed her face into the tiles. She heard the boots padding away, the sound of cloth and grunting breath as others sank to the floor. Voices passed overhead, echoing against the walls. Her heart pounded like thunder in her ears.

"Stay calm, my friends, stay calm," the pistol-man said with a hint of a foreign accent. "Reach for nothing until we tell you. We are pursuing a transaction with this bank."

"You think you'll get away with this? Sheriff will be here any minute. He probably already knows you're here—"

"What the alarm?" one of the gunmen drawled. "Yeah, we cut that. All them wires. Law ain't coming, pal."

A voice cut across, quiet and precise. "Enough. Ten minutes. Fill the bags."

From behind the counter, metal hinges squeaked. Frightened breathing rang out harsh against the brick walls. Anna lay stiff and sore on the cold marble, coat draped over her body, her satchel half-twisted under her, the strap digging into her neck. She was trying to decide what to do next. There was no way out that she could see, except keep to still, keep quiet; let them finish and go. But the dark double-holes of the shotgun hung invisible over her head. What if they didn't go? What if the sheriff came and there was shooting? She was helpless, lying there unable to even see the men above her. If she could just glimpse what was going on—

"Doing well, doing well everyone. We will be gone soon! Just a little longer."

"—think for one second you'll get to spend that money? County judge is a hanging judge, and he'll hang you—"

"Jesus Christ, pal, shut up. Time?"

"Seven minutes."

Heavy boots paced by Anna's line of sight. Her elbows ached where they'd hit the floor, the pain throbbing up her arms. She felt lightheaded. Her breath raced fast and shallow. She was sprawled out on a bank floor, guns overhead and hard men holding them, men she could barely see. A quick look from under her hat. A quick look and back down, just to take stock, just to plan—she could risk that, couldn't she? Just to know?

For a moment she warred with herself. Then she tilted her head up.

Three men clustered by the counter, one of them scooping handfuls of cash into a sack, the pistol-man watching the guard, the big one in heavy boots finishing his patrol of the line. The man in the long greatcoat stood against the opposite wall, rifle under one arm, his coat buttoned up tight as if against a chill. A gold pocket watch was clenched in one gloved hand. His eyes glittered beneath the cavalry hat, flat and cold as the marble tiles. He stood so still and silent that Anna caught herself staring, waiting to see if he would breathe.

Their eyes met. For a moment the flat gaze held her; then the rifle made a small gesture, almost mild. She read it and dropped her head back down, squeezing her eyes shut. None of her business. None of her business. None of her—

"Alright," the pistol-man said. "You have all been good! Now we come along and check your pockets. When our man comes to you, please reach slowly behind to remove your valuables. We accept jewelry, wallets. You may keep your checks. Attempt to rise and we will, I'm sorry to say, shoot you."

She lay there, breathing, listening to the brief mutters and whines of muffled protest. Boots slapped against the tile. The sounds grew louder and closer, vibrating along the marble beneath her. A toe nudged her shoulder out of the dark. "Pay up, darlin'."

"Llst—" Anna's tongue stuck to the roof her mouth. She swallowed, tried again. "Listen. I would. But—"

"No buts, girl. Just dip into that bag you got, nice and easy, and we'll all get on with our day. Don't make me search you."

Anna shook her head. "I don't have anything. No money. Don't carry any."

"If that's true, why the hell you even come to the bank?"

"I had to see a man about a ghost," Anna said.

"Shouldn't joke about that, ma'am. No you should not." Cloth whispered as the man knelt in front of her. Her satchel jerked as he rummaged through it, the strap yanking against her shoulder. A moment later Anna felt his hand patting down her coat, quick and business-like, rougher as he checked her hip pockets. "Nothing," he said, louder. "Just a bent silver dollar, a bunch of dried weeds and gewgaws. A damn hillbilly girl is all."

"Fine. Let's go. Three min—"

Hinges creaked behind her. "Folks, the sheriff just sent me over to—Jesus!"

A gunshot rang out, deafening. Someone screamed. A thud, a body hitting the floor, a squeak on the tiles, then another two shots, the sound bouncing off the walls, merging into a roar.

Someone seized Anna by the arm and hauled her to her feet, pressing a gun to the side of her head as they dragged her toward the door. She went easily, stunned, catching flashes as she went; one of the money bags dropping, spilling out cash; the guard covering his head, flat on the floor; a teller's staring eyes—

Her feet slipped and knocked on the tiles, bumped against the threshold. The sensation brought her back to herself, and suddenly she was struggling, elbows snapping out, snatching for the door frame. Someone cuffed her hard across the face and she was dragged out into the fall sunlight, the air fresh and crisp against her skin.

Hands took hold of her, pulled her aloft into a saddle. "Go, goddamnit, get her up!"

"Hold on, ma'am," came the pistol-man's voice from in front of her, sharp. "We will go fast, fairly fast. You wouldn't like to fall and crack your head, would you?"

Anna clung tight to him, dazed. The horse stirred under her. The smell of smoke was thick in the air, the sound of shouting ringing out from blocks away. Then the horse was moving, the gunmen peeling off and away from the First National Bank, Bakersmont Branch, galloping past the the new telegraph lines, past the people scattering on the street. The last buildings fell away into sloping fields, the grass blurring in the noonday light, and the blue-green swells of the hills spread out to receive them.

***

Half an hour after the robbery, Sheriff Martin Starks wiped a smear of soot from his face with a handkerchief and walked into the bank. He was a short man, with a blond mustache and watery eyes, his star carefully polished on his jacket. He wound his way through clumps of irate customers and settled himself against the long counter, leaning back to survey the room, keeping his face professional. Folks would be wound up, likely to shout. Starks did not care to be shouted at so early in the day. Better to look like he had a handle on things.

The bank manager spotted him and made a beeline across the tile, face thunderous. Starks met him halfway, clapped a hand on his shoulder. "This is a mess, Cy, a real mess. Grabbed one of your customers and all your money. How much they get?"

"Over seven thousand. Didn't clear us out, thank God, and they didn't shoot any customers or staff, which I'm glad of. After this there's a fellow or two I'd like to take out behind the woodshed myself."

They both looked over at the guard, a big, slab-faced man puffing himself up next to a deputy, his hand chopping down on his open palm as he spoke.

"I'm sure he did his best," Starks said, bland.

A vein twitched in the manager's forehead. "Maybe. You took your own sweet time, Martin, I don't mind saying."

"Well, Cyrus," Starks said, "It's been a busy morning. They set fire to a shop a few streets down, and I imagine they came straight here while we dealt with that. And that fancy new alarm of yours never rang. I just sent Deputy Howard by to look in on things on the off-chance. He's fine, by the way. Bullet took a chunk out of his arm. I just thought I'd see how he was doing before I came by. You don't mind, do you?"

The man pressed his lips together so tight they nearly disappeared, took a breath. "No. Of course not. The alarm was cut, by the way. Heaven only knows how. We only had it wired up a few months back. Martin, I can't see how this matters. Are you going after them at some point? Today, perhaps?"

Starks smiled. "I hear they lit out of here fast and went up into the hills. And you know, we won't run them down that way, 'cause the hills go on a ways, and there's trails through them aplenty. Where they went after town's anyone's guess until we get someone along who can follow a good sign. I'm sure they left one, running horses along like that. And if they did leave one, then there's plenty of time for me to do my job. You wait here in case I need to talk to you."

Starks left him there and went over to the deputy, a stocky young man studying a smear of blood on the marble tiles, a sheaf of wanted posters tucked under one arm. He clapped the guard on the shoulder, cutting him off in mid-flow. "Walk me through it, Joe."

"Five men come in about ten," the deputy said. "Held the place up, made everyone get down, shoved a gun barrel through the grate and told the tellers to open up the vault and fill the bags. They were on their way out when Howard came in. They took him by surprise, I guess, but he got a couple shots off as he went down. Didn't hit anything, but spooked 'em. They grabbed a girl and made a run for it. How's Howard?"

"Doctor says he'll scar up," Starks said. "Everyone here that was here?"

"A few folks ran out after the robbers did—"

"Any of the employees?"

"Most of them stayed. Except the washboy, Boyce Herriman. Manager sent him home before we got here, on account of he was shaking so bad."

"Well gee, I wish he hadn't done that," Starks said. "The kid might've seen something. And someone's gonna have to mop up the blood."

Joe shrugged. "Bobby's been taking testimonies from all the rest, and I showed 'em all our old posters, see if we could get an sense of who to look for. They had their faces covered, but we got two by the way they talked. One of 'em came in twirling a pistol and talking fancy, had kind of a foreign sound, like the notices said. Luke Pataki, I think. An East Coast stick-up man." He pulled out a poster and showed it to Starks, a slender-faced man with a neat, dark mustache.

"And the other?"

Joe rumpled the posters around and found out another, this one of a craggy face, one eye scarred, with a heavy beard. "Montague Giacomo. He beat a strikebreaker to death up in Pennsylvania and blew up a foreman's house. Anarchist. There's another some folks pointed to, but it don't sound right to me."

"Pass it over," Starks said.

The deputy handed him the paper and he squinted at it. "Jack 'Blackbone' Diggs," he readd. "Robbed six banks, killed near fifteen people when this was printed. Always leads a crew. Didn't the papers have him dead a few years back? I swear I heard that."

"So did I," Joe said. "So I didn't like to say."

"Well, I'll say," the guard said, unable to keep his silence. "I saw him. Blue coat and hat, and he had those dead eyes like the papers said. He didn't say much but he was in charge, sure enough. I could tell. We gonna saddle up, Sheriff? I'd like to get my hands on them."

"He's a hard man, if it is him," Starks said, examining the paper, thinking: harder than you for sure, son. Maybe harder than me, too. He cut eyes at the other deputy, caught his attention and waved him over. "But anyone can wear a greatcoat and a cavalry hat, and that old dime-novel hogwash don't happen so easily nowadays. Son, walk over there a moment, would you?"

The guard went. Starks lowered his voice, stepping closer to the deputies. "I gave Cy a hard time about it, but I just can't see how they cut that wire without help in here. Maybe one of the tellers. When Mark's all bandaged up, let's get him talking to them. See if we can shake something loose. And we need someone with a good head for track—"

He stopped, looking over at the opposite wall. A battered satchel and walking stick lay where the panelling met the marble floor, like someone had kicked it over there in a hurry. "What's that?"

Joe looked over at the other deputy and shrugged. "It was there when we came in."

Starks blew out a breath. Joe and Bobby were good boys, raised on the mountain and crack shots because of it. You had to forgive them little things like this. "I mean, whose it belong to?"

The guard bobbed back over, hound-dog eager to be of use. "Some girl came in before the robbers. Kind of thin and dirty, wearing a hat and coat that didn't fit right, and she had that bag and stick—"

"This the girl they dragged out?" Starks said.

"That's her," the guard said. "She was acting strange, looking around like she'd never been in a bank before. I kept my eye close on her in case she tried anything."

"Well, that's good," Starks said, all dry. "She might've robbed the place. Joe, run on down to the courthouse and let 'em know we need folks to gather up. Same to you, Bobby. Time to break out the rifles before Cy bites my ear off."

"Yes, Sheriff."

"Oh, Joe?" Starks said, looking at the bag. "Tell Breden to bring the dogs."

***

When the pistol-man bound her wrists behind the narrow ash tree, Anna kept still and let him. He favored her with a quick smile as he came back around, his neat mustache pulling up at his lips. Then he nodded and went back to join the others a few feet down the slope.

The gunmen had ridden into the late afternoon, fast at first, crossing the slopes of the foothills and splashing down into a muddy creek to throw off the scent. They cut up a narrow trail, the horses picking their way over the seeps, past thick lilac and rhododendron and into a shallow, shaded notch halfway up the ridgeline. It was a thirty-foot shelf of flat ground, broken by long walls of folded rock jutting out of the dirt. A tumble of huge boulders formed a rough shelter of to the side, a little spring trickling out of the base and running down along wet masses of leaves and mossy stones.

Mosquitos whined around her face. She sat there, the bark hard against her aching shoulders, taking stock. The shock of her capture had drained away during the ride, enough for her to start thinking. While her blood was up she'd pictured herself leaping off the horse, or reaching for the pistol-man's gun as they rode. But running was out of the question, and he was bigger than her, a hard man, a killer; even if she got her hands on his pistol, she'd never fired one before. And there were four other men besides. Her stick and satchel were gone, the salt back up by the grave, the silver coin and poultices lying somewhere on the bank floor.

There was panic hiding in that thought, so she breathed out, slow, and slid it away. Her tools wouldn't help here in any case. Nothing to do now but keep still and watch.

Pale yellow clouds streaked the sky overhead, the blue shadows deepening beneath the leaves. The gunmen moved quickly in the cool light, stripping the saddles off their mounts and dropping the bags. The cash was poured out, counted, sorted into shares and tucked away in respective saddle-bags, leaving a last pile on the ground. One of the men—lanky, sandy haired—fetched a shovel from up in the rocks and begin digging at the base of a nearby tree.

The pistol-man sat nearby, cheek working over a strip of jerky, his neat face thoughtful. "Six thousand," he said. "That could have been worse. I would go far as to say it went well."

"You think it goes well anytime you get to talk." The big gunman settled with a grunt a few feet away, laying his shotgun beside him and crossing his big boots. He was bearded, the curls black and wiry on his chin; a puckered scar ran across one brow. "You'd say mass at a shotgun wedding."

The pistol-man gave an elegant little shrug. "I am a loss to the stage."

The spadehead rang, glancing off chunks of stone in the dirt. "Christ, this dirt's half-rock. I don't see why I gotta be the one to dig it out. It's his share."

"Want to take that up with him, Josiah?"

"I do not."

The fourth man came back around from around the rocks, buttoning his trousers. Anna had no experience with him and so had nothing to go on; nothing but a buckskin coat, inexpertly made, and his broken nose and hungry eyes. "Does hurt to see that cash going in the dirt."

"It goes where I say it goes."

The last man sat in the shade under the boulders, his faded blue greatcoat still buttoned tight, his scarf wadded under his chin. There was a cruel architecture to the face under the cavalry hat; sharp and heavy as a hatchet, the skin hanging slack off the bone. Big hands crossed over his belt, the knuckles webbed in scars. His stillness ate at her. As in the bank, she was gripped with the sudden conviction that she could watch him all night and never see him move.

Josiah piled up the remaining cash, scooped it into a sack and deposited it in the hole. Sighed, grabbed the shovel and began spooning dirt and bits of rock back over it. "Got to say, I do agree with Luke. Anytime I get don't get shot is a good day."

"Wouldn't have gotten shot at if your kid had cut the wire," the man in the buckskin said. "The law still showed."

"He cut the wire," Josiah said. "He swore up and down he did, and he wouldn't lie to me. And if he *hadn't* cut that wire, the law would have come down immediately, not sent a man to look in. That's just bad luck. Maybe it was the fire that tipped 'em off."

"The kid's slow in getting here," the big man said.

"He's got a couple hundred set aside for him and knows it. He'll come."

The man in the buckskin fished around in a pocket, pulled out a wad of chewing tobacco and stuffed it in his mouth. "We planning on giving him a share? Seems easier just to put him in a ditch. Can't squawk that way. Speaking of—"

Tied to her tree, Anna went very still.

"Speaking of," said the man in the buckskin said, "What are we going to do about her? She's seen our faces."

The men looked around at her, raising their eyebrows like they'd forgotten she was there. Mostly they were frowning, like they were running back over their conversation, trying to remember what they'd said. But there was a gleam now in the face of the man in buckskin, a gleam Anna didn't like at all.

"You know," Luke said. "I assume we are keeping her in case the law catches up. They are less likely to shoot that way. But now I am not so sure they will catch up. We have a long head start on them, and this is rough country."

Josiah flicked something off his shirt. "Any point in keeping her?"

"Ask her."

They flinched at the quiet, precise voice, all of them, and at the sound that followed, a click that echoed off the rocks: the sound of a round being chambered into a rifle. Pebbles crunched under worn boots. The man in the greatcoat was on his feet now, moving with steady, smooth purpose, the barrel loose in his hands. "Why should we keep you around?"

"You can let me go," Anna said. The pain in her shoulder had turned sharp, pins and needles running down her arms, but she didn't dare shift with them looking at her. "I've been quiet this whole time, and I can keep quiet."

"That's not the choice." The angular face tilted under the cavalry hat. "The choice is, we keep you around, or we don't. Why should we keep you around?"

"I—" she stared at him, nonplussed. Sweat dripped down her face. "I don't follow."

"You don't follow. What's your name?"

"A—Anna. O'Brien."

"What value are you, Anna O'Brien? If you're valueless… then what should be done with you?"

She looked at him, utterly at a loss for words. His eyes were locked on her, a dull glint, utterly without pity. Eyes like the shotgun barrel, pulling her in, promising to snuff her out. She opened her mouth, closed it, opened it again. Watched the rifle rise, the eyes above it glinting, glinting like—

"Gold!" she said. "Wait! *Wait!* I know where the gold is!"

"Horseshit," Josiah said. "She said she didn't have anything in the bank. Now she's got gold?"

The flat eyes looked at Josiah and he shut up, stepped back and stared at the ground. Then they were back on her. "What gold?"

Anna forced herself to breathe. "Gold...nobody'll miss. Buried in a forgotten graveyard. Someone's family inheritance. I was supposed to let them know, but..." she looked at all of them and shook her head. "It's free gold. Nobody's looking for it. Nobody alive knows it's there but me."

"I want you to understand me," the man said. "Before you answer my next questions, I want to be… clear. My name is Blackbone Jack Diggs. And you will tell me the truth. How much gold is there?"

"A coffin's worth," Anna said. "I think. I didn't… get a whole look at it. I was just told to let someone know it was there."

"And who," Blackbone said, quiet, "told you do that?"

That brought her up short. She wobbled there a moment, trying to think through her next step. Who told her? What if he thought she was joking? But she'd already said that nobody alive knew about the gold, hadn't she? A voice inside her whispered, soft and urgent; *it'll be worse if he thinks you're lying.* "A ghost," she said. "I'm a… a conjure woman. I settle ghosts sometimes. I was trying to settle this one when it told me."

"A ghost!" The man in buckskin laughed, a high cackle that petered out and died in the still air. Nobody else smiled.

"And where do we find this… ghost gold?"

She had to move carefully now, very carefully. "A day out from Bakersmont."

He considered her, his face hard and shadowed, dead still. "You want to play it that way?"

"Yes," Anna said.

"We could hurt you," said the man in the buckskin. "You'd sing different then, wouldn't you? All kinds of things."

Anna kept her eyes on Blackbone. "You could hurt me. But if you do, I'll tell you every place I ever visited, tell you, tell you *anything* to get you to stop. You know that, right? You can search them all and never know which it was. There's a lot that's day out from Bakersmont. And you don't want to spend much time out there looking."

The bark dug into her shoulders. Blackbone looked at her with his strange flat eyes, and the men around him stared at the two of them, watchful, like cats studying a catamount, waiting to see what would happen.

"You'll take us there in the morning. Show us the grave," Blackbone said at last. "If there's gold there… we'll let you go. There's not, I'll put a bullet in you and put you in that coffin. You lead the law to us, I'll do worse. That square?"

Square? She wanted to laugh. They would probably kill her at the grave either way. If she said no, they would certainly kill her now. It was an extra day, that was all: a day to maybe find a way to wiggle out from under them. She knew it, and she knew without looking that everyone else knew it, too. But what else was there?

"Yeah," Anna said. "That's square."

Blackbone nodded. Then he turned on his heel and left them all there, walking back up into the shadows beneath the boulders, settling himself back down until he was just one more grey shape among the folds of rock, still as the surrounding stone. The men watched him go, looking at one another, their faces grim. Then Josiah shuddered and spat on the ground.

"What I want to know is," he said, "where's that damn kid?"

***

Boyce was still picking his way over the stream when the figure appeared from the gloom behind the nearest tree. He jumped, a skinny sixteen-year-old in a cotton shirt and suspenders, his hair up in a cowlick, jumped because he thought it was the sheriff, the law, a whole posse hiding behind a tree for him, Boyce Herriman. Then he recognized the man and scowled. "Josiah! Christ. What'd you go and do that for? You scared the shit out of me."

"You're late," Josiah said. "Were you followed?"

"No, I slipped on out fine." Cold water was soaking into Boyce's shoes, and he shifted up onto a mossy rock. "Mr. Cyrus sent me home right after you left, on account of I's shaking so bad. I just wandered around a bit 'fore I came up, to make sure. Was that alright?"

Josiah just looked at him, shaking his head. The sandy-haired man had come into the bank a week back, dressed in a clean shirt and trousers. He'd struck up a conversation with Boyce, a conversation that led to a drink in the bar, the man paying, and soon the conversation was Boyce staring at his drink and spilling out his frustrations. How his family had sold the homeplace when he was a child, come down to town with a parcel of money, until his daddy drank it away and they ended up in a shack in the hills outside of town, Boyce mopping floors and polishing up in the bank, watching people move more money in a day than he'd ever see. And it wasn't fair, was it? And Josiah had smiled at him, friendly, and said you know, Boyce, I wanted to talk to you about that—-

So he cut the alarm for them. He'd heard the manager talking about it a few months back, had taken a vague interest, enough to keep an eye out when he cleaned for the wire that ran along the panelling back behind the counter. After his conversation with Josiah he came in early one day with a spade, looked over his shoulder, and cut it, toeing the two strands over each other so they looked like they were still connected. Stuck the spade in his pail of water like it was a mop and walked it back to the broom closet, took it out with him when he left. When the robbers hit the bank he was in the back, suddenly afraid at the sound of gunshots, thinking about how it might go wrong, how they'd give him up if they got caught. But then the manager came through looking like someone had hit him over the head, saw him shaking and told him to get out of his sight. So that had been all right.

Now Josiah beckoned him to follow, leading him across the little stream and up into the notch in the hillside, around boulders that loomed up like moss-draped walls in the evening shadows. Horses stirred where they were tied to the trees. Down in the notch the robbers had gathered around the red coals of a small fire, except for one of them who sat off a ways, dark and still under the tumble of rocks. There was a girl there too, Boyce saw with surprise, sitting bound to a sapling, pretty, her strong face set and watchful beneath a broad-brimmed hat.

Boyce looked at her until Josiah clapped him on the shoulder, spun him around, and pressed a few bills into his hand. He looked at them, face falling. "That's it?"

"Christ," Josiah said. "That's $200 in your hand. That's plenty."

"Only I heard you took six thousand," Boyce said. "Mr. Cyrus said before he sent me home. Six thousand, and five of you, and me. I figure I'm short $800."

"The way that law man came in and we had to draw down, you're lucky you're getting anything at all. Hell, we don't even know you cut the damn wire."

"I cut it!" Boyce said, stung. "You couldn't have done it if I didn't. Way I see it, that gets me—"

"Share's $300 for cutting the wire," said the man under the rocks, quiet. "Less a hundred for the law man. That's all you get. Prove yourself, you get more. Or go."

"What you think about that, Boyce?" Josiah had a hand on his shoulder again, led him over to the fire and pushed him down onto the leaves. "You gonna go home? Or you want to live tough a while? Earn more?"

"Boyce?" the woman said. "Boyce Herriman?"

Boyce flinched and looked over at her, guarded all of a sudden. "No," he said. "That ain't me."

"Sure it is," said a broken-nose man in a buckskin jacket. His cheek worked and he spat over his shoulder. "Don't need to worry about her. She's gonna be real nice to us, lead us to a whole bunch of gold, and if she doesn't we'll kill her. Might kill her anyway. You can't be an outlaw and be scared of your own name."

Boyce laughed, suddenly uncertain. Outlaw was a big word and he liked how it fit him, but he wasn't sure about killing. "Yeah," he said. "Yeah, I'm him. What of it?"

The woman shook her head, looking at him, then tilted her eyes up into the dark and closed them. "Nothing. Just met someone asking after you."

He watched her a moment, looking at the curve of her legs in her trousers. The men around the fire grinned at each other and he grinned too, slow. An outlaw. He could see it: make some more money, go east somewhere, live high. He looked at the guns sitting at their sides, shotguns and pistols nestled in the leaf-litter. "I get a gun?"

"Sure," said the big man with the scarred face. "When you buy one."

They cooked up a pot of red beans on the fire, using rhododendron leaves as bowls and eating with their fingers. Boyce knew Josiah, and he picked up the other names fast: Rainey in his buckskin, big scarred Montague and dapper Luke, who gave him a smile that felt warmer than the others. He listened while they talked, about other jobs and brushes with the law out in the territories, narrow escapes. The whole time he kept silent, thinking, sneaking looks over at the girl.

"You thinking about her gold?" Rainey said, and laughed a high, sharp little laugh. "You ever had gold from a woman like that? I bet you never have. Maybe she'd give it to you, though, 'for we have to shoot her. Here, you see she just got the one leg under those pants? A wooden leg. You think she takes it off? What you think that's like?"

Boyce looked back at the fire, his cheeks flushing. Beside him, Luke frowned over his neat mustache. "A lady has her secrets."

"I never knowed a one who could keep 'em." Rainey spat over his shoulder again, turned back to the fire. "We'll have to kill her, you know. Whatever Blackbone says. Hell, she's seen our faces. Sitting there all quiet, looking at us."

Josiah grinned. "I don't reckon she's looking at you."

"He's right, though," Montague said.

"Christ, Monty, what harm can she do? I don't like thinking about shooting a cripple girl like that. I'll drop a man, sure, but a woman—"

"You yellow?" Rainey said. "That it? Hell, I'll do her. This were my crew, I'd beat the gold out of her, first, then I'd—"

"Well, Rainey, it's not your crew," Luke said, polite. "Is it?"

They were all silent at that. Frogs called in the dark, and the coals pulsed, dim and dying in the firepit. Boyce looked away as the silence stretched, looked over to where the shadow sat, silent on the rocks. "What about Blackbone? He ain't cold?"

"No," Montague said. Beside him, Josiah stared into the fire, his jaw working.

"He don't talk much," Boyce said, pressing a little. "Do he?"

They looked at him, and at each other. Then Luke sighed and leaned forward. "You want to know about Blackbone Jack?"

"Sure," Boyce said.

"I don't know him well," Luke said. "I met him a few years back out west and we worked together a few times. Just in passing, you understand? He was a different man, then. Good for a smile or two, and he would come and sit at the fire at night. When I joined up with him again this spring, he was like this. Not warm. I think something must have happened to him in the time between."

"He just got hard," Monty said. "I used to smile more, too. But you have a company man break a shovel on your back, and you watch your friends drop dead in the mine for less than a dollar a day, and the government stamping down on you when you try to fight back—"

"Monty," Luke said.

"I'm just saying that life changes a man." For a moment the big man's voice came out low and regretful. The scar was a black canyon across the crags of his face. "Makes him drill down on the thing he knows how to do. Life does that."

"No, don't go easy on him," said Josiah. "He's gonna run with us, he needs to know the rest. Tell him what you told us."

Luke looked over his shoulder and lowered his voice, so that Boyce had to lean forward to hear him. Out of the corner of his eye he saw the tied-up woman craning her head a little, listening.

"I do not say this is true," Luke said. "I heard it from a man, who knew another man. Hearsay, you know? But he told me that Blackbone came east a few years back and ran a few jobs with his old band, up in Kentucky. Like I said, I worked with them once or twice, and they were bad men. How Blackbone kept them in line, I don't know. Except that one day, maybe, he could not. I heard that they turned on him, cut him open, and left his body in the high country, took his share."

"Cut him open?" Boyce said. The night's cold was pressing in, and he put his hands closer to the red coals.

"I suppose they wanted to be sure. One of them was caught by the law, later on, and told them Blackbone was done for before they hanged him. It was in the papers. Another was found out in the woods some time later. They thought perhaps a bear had gotten him. Terrible mess. And another I am told died very badly indeed, though how, the man did not like to say. What happened to the rest, I do not know. Blackbone came back in any case, so I suppose if they did leave him, he was not as dead as they thought."

Josiah shook his head. "You got it right in front of you, Luke, and you won't see it. I been up in the hills my whole life, got a sense for things. He ain't just quiet. That man is—"

"Professional," Montague said. "He's professional, and he's good at his business, whatever he is. He squeezes the bastards where it hurts. And you get paid. So no more ghost stories. Shut your mouth and let it be."

Josiah's mouth tightened and he stood. "I gotta piss."

"You have to understand," Luke said to Boyce after a moment, after Josiah had faded away into the dark. "He is a professional. That is... all he is. You can stay by him until you've made your money, and then go. I am headed back to New York after this, you know? He will not stop you. I don't believe he will even notice you are gone. He himself, he will not stop. Not ever. Make some money and then go, and keep out of his way."

"I would have just shot him," Rainey said into his chest, quiet and hard. "It were me, I would have shot him in the head. Three bullets. Man doesn't get up from that."

"I would not like to try," Luke said. "I'm going to bed. You have first watch, Monty?"

"Yeah."

"I don't...I don't have a bedroll," Boyce said.

Montague eyed him. "Then it'll be a hard night for you."

The last thing Boyce saw before he closed his eyes up against the hollow of a tree was the girl watching from her tree, her face a band of shadow beneath the hat, her head tilted toward the rocks. Nothing moved in the dark where Blackbone sat. Nothing at all.

***

When the voice came out of the night it caught Anna dozing, jerked her in her bonds. Silver moonlight striped the floor of the notch, picking out leaves and rocks and the huddles of sleeping men. She was weary. Bone-weary. Her shoulders had gone numb, and the night chill was in her, making her shiver. She'd tried once or twice to lean her head back, to go to sleep. But though her eyelids fluttered they always came open again, tracking over until they came to rest on the shadows of the boulders, where a pair of still boots were crossed in the moonlight.

"I feel your eyes on me," Blackbone said. "You believe those stories they told?"

Anna said nothing.

"You're not… deaf." The voice was different than before, harsher, pausing in unexpected places, like its owner had to stop and draw breath. And you're not asleep. Anna… O'Brien. If you did believe those stories. What would you do?"

"Why would I do anything?"

"Everyone has to do something. Doing nothing is… doing something. You say you settle ghosts. A conjure woman. If you believed those stories… what would you do? Would you settle me?"

"Is it true they cut you up?"

"Yeah," came the voice from the rocks. "That's true."

Anna stared into the night, at the other men bundled up on the floor of the notch, at the Herriman boy huddled in a tree hollow. One of the band was posted up across from the boulders, keeping watch: but his head was down, his face hidden in shadow. No owls hooted, no crickets, no frogs calling. The moonlight silvered all of it, froze it silent and still. "Did you die?"

"I got… cold, down inside. Cold where the knives went when they opened me up and left me. Then nothing. Nothing worth waiting for. Nothing worth… being dead for. So I got up. You can do that, you know. If you want it enough… Would you want it enough?"

"I don't know," Anna said.

"You don't know," whispered the voice. Not like it was mocking her, and not like it agreed. Not like anything.

The lattice of shadows swirled on the ground. Anna's heart pulsed. Something rose up inside her, and she turned from it, turned to look at the crossed boots jutting out of the dark. "Why do this?" she said. "I saw them bury your share. What do you want the money for?"

"For?" There was a glimmer of something in Blackbone's voice at last, like she'd asked an unanswerable question. "I don't want it for anything. I just want it. I want… it. Why didn't you take the gold?"

"I'm out on the road. If I had it, if I met someone like—like—

" "When you knew the gold was there… Nobody looking for it. Did your fingers itch? Did you think about all the things you could do with the money? Did you think about keeping it? Did you think about the hole inside you and how you'd fill it?"

Anna's voice was small in the dark. "It wasn't mine."

"But it could have been. You looked at it and it could have been. You were scared of it… and you ran. Scared of what it meant to have it. Because you think there's something else. But there's nothing else."

She said nothing.

"You don't understand. I didn't understand until it happened to me. You want to see it?"

"What?"

The boots shifted, dragging back into the dark. Leather rasped on stone. It came out of the black and into the moonlight, step by dragging step. Scarred fingers on the buttons of the greatcoat, popping them open one by one. The eyes glinted under the cavalry hat, glinting like cold stars, dead light, glinting out of the hard, slack face. "You want to see the place… they cut me open?"

His fingers undid the last button.

Later, she was never able to describe what it was that she'd seen there, under the greatcoat. Just something pulling her in, the howl of cold wind and the sound of a body dropping, kicking and gurgling on the rocks, opened up, open and waiting for something to crawl inside. She looked and opened her mouth, but the scream would not come, not as Blackbone Jack came toward her, staring, holding his coat open, the force of him suffocating her, sucking in the world…

Her eyes snapped open. There was a hand on her mouth and a gun pressed against her head, a pistol. She strained against her bonds, eyes wide.

"Don't say nothing," Boyce Herriman said a low voice. "I'm taking you out of here and we're gonna see about that gold. Just the two of us, just you and me. Won't that be nice?"

***

He wouldn't have started thinking about it if Rainey hadn't told him to keep watch. The broken-nosed man woke Boyce from a fitful sleep by kicking his leg, saying he was tired, and if Boyce wanted to prove himself he could start by taking Rainey's shift. So Boyce got up, stiff, and went over to lean against a tree.

He stepped from foot to foot, shivering a little, staring out into the dark until he got bored. So he started looking across the notch, at the girl. Looking at her and thinking about her and her gold, gold only she knew how to find. That got him mulling over the way the other robbers—the way Rainey—looked at her, the way they'd shorted him his share of the bank money, when he'd been the one to cut that wire, tucked back behind the counter where they couldn't get it...

So he took Luke's pistol and holster from where it lay by his bedroll and went to fetch her. Mouth dry, he untied her hands and led her away toward the horses, motioned at her to wait while he fetched a saddle and bridle, moving as quietly as possible. He picked the animal that looked calmest and saddled it, boosted the girl up. Then he untied it and led it away through the loamy soil on foot, going down the slope the way they had come, away from the notch.

When they crossed the creek Boyce lit a lamp, pushed the girl forward on the saddle and climbed up behind her. He'd been thinking she'd be relieved, might even melt back into him, soft. But she held herself stiff away from his body, and her words came out tense and quiet. "You know the big timber tract north of Bakersmont?"

"I come from that way originally," he said, whispering back like the night was listening. "Ain't been back since they took the property. "

"You know how to get there?"

He nodded before realizing she couldn't see him. "Guess so."

"Go that way."

It took a bit of time. Boyce had ridden before, here and there during the field season, and vaguely recalled how to do it. But the horse didn't know him and had to be coaxed into following his directions. Eventually he let the horse choose its own path, until they lucked onto a narrow trail going what seemed to him the right way. They picked along a while in the dark, neither speaking, the night velvet black under the branches even with the lamp. Then the trees fell away and the moonlight shone on the hardpack logging road, winding like a snake down into the long, shallow valley.

Boyce looked back over his shoulder as the horse went out onto the open dirt, straining his eyes for any sign of pursuit. One hand dropped to the gun at his hip, to reassure himself of its weight. But nothing moved in the dark behind them. With nobody on watch, the robbers would sleep until morning, wouldn't they? More than enough time for a good head start.

In front of him in the saddle the girl shifted, rolling her shoulders so that he heard them click under her coat.

"You all right?"

"Sore," she said.

"We're making good time," he said.

She didn't respond to that. Boyce wondered if she was nervous like he was nervous, low and whispering in the back of his head. He urged the horse into a quicker trot. "You know," he said, "I don't reckon they can be after us all that fast. They got to pick their way down, same as us, even if they do it in the morning. Might not even come after us at all. They got plenty of money, right?"

He remembered Luke's voice suddenly, the funny accent. *He will not stop. Not ever.* Shivered there on the horse, suddenly, looked back behind him again. Nothing. The reins clammy in his hands. "Here," he said. "You think he's really..."

Under her coat, the girl's shoulders grew tighter in the lamplight. "Did you see him get up? Before you woke me?"

"No," Boyce said. "He's all still when I come and got you. Why?"

"Nothing," the girl said, not sounding like she believed it. "Just... just a dream."

"I figure—" Boyce chewed on it. "I figure he can't be like they said. He's walking around, talking. He can't be a haint. What's a haint want with cash, anyhow? They tell some stories about him, but that don't make him a haint. Hell, I got a gun now. If he tries to follow us I'll just—I'll shoot him. Takes more'n ghost stories to scare me."

She said nothing to that either. He tried to tuck an arm around her, wondering if she'd relax into him now, but her body stayed rigid under him, pushed up against the saddle horn. So he fell silent too, a hard and mulish silence. Maybe he wouldn't share the gold with her like he'd been thinking. See how she liked that.

The light crept slow and watery over the ridges. The forest fell away behind them as they came down the road into the valley, sudden as if they'd passed through a green picket of branches. Ahead stretched a landscape of wrinkled grey, faint in the half-light, but not softened by it: tree trunks tilting like gravestones in the brittle earth, row upon row of them, thickets of briar and low brush clutching their sides. The breeze gusted over the washed-out gullies, dry and smelling of dust.

"Jesus." Boyce stared at it from horseback, shaking his head, mouth slack. "I never—I never knowed it to look so bad. They took all of it."

The girl looked over her shoulder, and he was struck by how close her face was to his own, the grey eyes sharp and steady, like she was weighing him. "How long your kin live out this way?"

After her silence the question surprised him. "Pa allowed once that Herrimans was here since forever and a day," he told her. "Came over before even there was a country. But we ain't had the papers to say so. Maybe ten years back, the company come with papers, told us to get off their land, paid us a bit to get rid of us. Did that to everyone living here. I was seven, maybe? We moved out to Bakersmont, but Pa never did take to it."

"Took it hard?"

"Drank himself dead," Boyce said, suddenly morose. "We close?"

She looked up ahead and pointed at a far-off section of slope, where shelves of rock poked out from the hillside. "That way."

They galloped down the road now, dust swirling in morning sunlight. Hoofbeats echoed against the dry ground. The awful emptiness of the place battered at Boyce, at his memories of cool green light and grass in the meadows, the clear bubble of creeks seeping from out of the rock, dragonflies flashing in the clearings. The streams they passed now were muddy and silted out, fringes of greenery clinging to their collapsing banks. He looked at them, thinking about the cash in the bank vault, the rumble of the trains in the depot. All that money and him living up above town in a shack, while they got rich cutting up Herriman land. Wasn't he owed something? What he could do with that gold…

The road ran up and around a fold in the slope, the length of the valley vanishing behind them. The rock shelves were dull grey in the light, cracked and weathered, stacked in long layers out of the eroding hillside. One ledge jutted out like a wall, the roadward side covered in a scree of boulders and slanting trees.

"Behind there," the girl said. They left the hard-packed dirt and dismounted, walking around the edge of the folded granite and down into a broad, sheltered swath of dirt, like a giant had taken a bite out of the slabs. Boyce tied the horse to a bush, looking at it. The sound of the wind was muffled here, the open side a vista of barren ground stretching to the north. Beneath a withered tangle of dogsbane and fern sat twenty faded headstones.

The girl made a noise in her throat and darted over to pluck up something from the weeds, a little pouch that vanished into her coat.

"What's that?" Boyce said.

"Salt," she said. "I left it earlier. See that gravestone that's half-snapped? That's where the gold is."

Boyce stared at the spot. His lips were dry suddenly, and he licked them and swallowed. There was a faint thundering in his ears. "If that don't beat all."

The girl gave him a serious nod. "I'm going now."

"What?"

"I was supposed to bring you," the girl said. She rolled her shoulders again, wincing, and wiped her forehead. "That's all."

"But I—" he looked at her, panicked, not sure what to say. Licked his lips again. "You know, I don't care you got one leg. I figure you and me could have a time with this gold, go down to Nashville, maybe. Why don't you stay, help me dig it up? What you think about that?"

Her grey eyes widened a little. "I… no, Boyce Herriman. No. That's not for me."

"Maybe Memphis?"

"Not anywhere," she said. "It's not my gold, and you aren't my… I'm going now. Best of luck to you.

"Why you so eager to go?"

"Because what happens next ain't my business," she said, tight. "I was supposed to bring you. You're here."

He looked at her stupidly, his face and ears hot. Then the rest of him was hot, too, red-hot, and he shook his head, feeling the weight of the gun at his side. "How do I know there's gold there, anyway? How do I know you ain't lying to me? You're gonna stay right here until I dig this up. Hell, maybe you should dig it up. You're the one claims it's there."

She edged away from him, wobbly, her hands opened up at her sides like she was thinking about running. "Boyce?"

"Dig it up," he shouted at her.

A note of frustration entered her voice. "With *what?*"

He'd forgotten to bring the spade. Boyce stared at her, looked at the ground, at the horse, feeling a fresh prickling wave of embarrassment roll over him. He looked up into her grey eyes and suddenly he hated her, hated her stony face and stiff body, hated the way she pressed away from him. Suddenly the gun was in his hand, cool metal pressing into his palm. "Think you're funny? They were gonna kill you. I took you away, and you won't even… won't even talk to me, don't even think to bring a spade, *stupid*…I guess you'll just have to, have to dig with your hands. How about that?"

"Boyce," the girl said, her voice very quiet. "Are you pointing that gun at me?"

"I am." He stepped forward, showing ti to her, and watched her shy backward. Behind him the horse wickered. "You see it? Got my finger in the trigger. Now dig, cause if you don't, I'll shoot you—"

Something thudded down on the dirt beside him. A spade, the blade glinting in the shaft of sunlight.

They both looked at it, eyes wide. A terrible cold feeling wormed inside Boyce. He saw the girl glance up, pale. Turned to face the granite shelf shielding them from the road, from the sounds of the road. Looked up the cracks and crevasses and hanging bushes, up at the rifle barrel pointing down at him, held by a man in a cavalry hat and a greatcoat. Montague and Luke emerging from the trees beside him, their faces set and hard.

"Josiah?" Luke's voice was curt.

"Hey, kid," the sandy-haired man said, easing around the edge of the granite wall, holding his pistol on them. Rainey followed, one eye swollen shut, lip caked in dry blood. "Dig or I'll shoot, huh? Sound like an outlaw now, pal. Couldn't have said it better."

The gun wavered in Boyce's hands and he darted his head around, trying to think. Kept looking back up at the hatchet face and the empty eyes, staring at him like he was an insect, a fly trapped under a gun barrel, buzzing, buzzing…

"You left a trail," came the quiet, cold voice from above. "People always do. You got greedy, thought I wouldn't… follow. But I always follow, Boyce."

"Please," Boyce said. "Please… "

"You wanted a shovel," Blackbone said. "There it is. Dig."

***

It was the sounds that bothered Anna most. The thump of the shovel in the dirt, the patter of soil on the growing mound. The hoarse sob of Boyce's breath in his throat. The soft rasp of a knife blade on wood.

She had spent most of the day in a strange half-doze, her sense of time broken under the mingled weight of tedium, terror, and a weariness so bone-deep she thought she might sink into the ground. Only the throbbing in her shoulders and needle-thin pain in her back kept her awake: that and the sound of the shovel crunching into the ground, a steady beat echoing off the rocks. Every bite from the blade bringing them closer to a coffin. Damn the gold, damn the ghost, damn the robbers, and damn Boyce Herriman most of all. She hoped they shot him.

Now early evening spilled over the rock ledges, the golden lines on the granite fading as the sun slipped beneath the ridges. Out on the slopes, the tree stumps melted into the gloaming. The men clustered around the rock wall, Luke and Montague playing cards around the lamp, Josiah sitting on the lip of the ledge, whittling. Rainey prowled around the open grave, his good eye glowering now down at Boyce, now at the rest of the men, cursing and kicking the boy's shoulders whenever he faltered.

Blackbone sat like a statue on a slab of granite, his expressionless face grotesque in the evening light. Anna looked at him sometimes and just as quickly looked away. The sight of him made her think of the thing under the greatcoat, made her chest clench and her stomach roll. It might have been a dream of him, up in the notch, just a dream. But the thought didn't calm her. If it was a dream, then he was a dead-eyed man with a rifle, and she had only a bag of salt in her pocket. And if it wasn't…

Again and again the shovel went down into the ground. Then it thumped on something, and went still.

Anna's breath caught in her throat. A cold breath drifted down the slope, rustling the dogsbane. The blade hit wood again, harder. Over by the rocks the men looked up, faces grey in the evening light.

"Don't stop now, boy." Rainey kicked Boyce in the shoulder, a quick, vicious strike of the boot. "Well? Let's see if you and your cripple girl got anything down there!"

Boyce choked out a breath, hammered the shovel down twice into the lid of the casket. Wood splintered. He swayed there a moment, holding onto the the lip of the hole for support, the dirt coming up to his armpits. The sound he made was somewhere between a gasp and a desperate laugh. "Shit. It's here. The gold's here."

"I'll be damned," Josiah said. He stood up on the ledge, craning his head for a better look. Below him, Luke rose with the lamp, Montague following, the weeds crunching under their feet as they came over.

Blackbone stood as well, swinging the rifle up over his shoulder and walking with purposeful speed out of the shadows. He settled back into stillness at the head of the grave. "How much?"

"It's...in bars." Boyce shook his head, the movement jerky. "It was here the whole time. All those hard days, and it was here. We could've—"

"You could have," Blackbone said. "Now it's ours. Count it."

Boyce drove the shovel down, twice more, until the coffin lid splintered and broke. He leaned down again, and this time he came up holding two gold bars. He dumped them on the rough cloth. Another gold bar clunked down beside it, and another, clinking like the shovel had clinked against chunks of rock. Boyce's breath sounded ragged in the silence. In the end, twenty-six bars lay glinting in the lamplight. Glinting like the setting sun.

"That's all," Boyce said. "That's all there is. The rest is…just... bones…"

"That is a beautiful thing," Luke said, examining them with the lamp. He set it down on the ground beside the gold. "Just beautiful."

Montague whistled. "Near an even split, too."

Anna breathed out, long, the hollow feeling inside her growing. She dug a hand in the dirt, clumps of dry soil falling through her fingers. They hadn't bothered to bind her hands, this time. Now that they were focused on the gold, could she sneak away, take one of the horses like Boyce had? Maybe. But the weeds were dry around her and they'd hear her as soon as she moved. The shotgun barrels hung in her vision, the rifle, holes in the world sucking everything in. They were going to kill her soon, she could feel it. Unless…

The last hint of light still glimmered on the ridgeline, a sliver against the purple sky. She stared at it, willing it to go down. Was it her imagination, or had something quivered under her fingers?

"Come up," Blackbone said.

Boyce scrabbled up out of the grave on trembling arms, his face muddy with sweat and grave-dust, his cowlick matted to his scalp. He lay on the ground for a moment, exhausted, hands blistered and raw. Then Rainey kicked him again and he pushed himself to his feet and stood swaying, backlit by the lamp. He looked at the gunmen around him like he was confused, and then down at the gold.

"You took my gun," Luke told him, voice clipped and serious. "And Rainey's horse. They deal roughly with horse thieves in the Territory. Do you know that?"

Boyce shook his head.

Blackbone came around the hole to stand in front of Boyce, the greatcoat hissing against his legs. Was he standing taller, now? Taller and wider, buttons shining and leading up toward the empty white face, a sharp skull pushing through the flesh. Inhuman. Behind him, the others stepped back. "Do you still have your share from the bank?"

"I'm...I'm sorry. I won't—-"

A gloved hand reached out. "Do you… have it?"

Slowly Boyce fumbled in his pocket and pulled out a wrinkled pair of bills, placing them in Blackbone's palm. They fluttered there in the breeze. Then the big fingers snapped tight around them, clenched them.

"Please, sir, please...I swear…"

"Which piece do you want?"

Boyce stared at him like an animal looking at a trap, baffled and terrified. Then, slowly, he relaxed, licked his parted lips, and looked down at the gold bars.

He was still looking at them when Blackbone put the rifle to the side of his head and pulled the trigger.

The crack of the gunshot thundered off the rocks, swallowing Anna's scream. A black spray arced across the lamp's glow. She jerked against the gravestone, ears ringing, watching Boyce's body topple backward into the hole he'd dug. As he disappeared something twisted under her feet, deep down.

Blackbone swung the rifle toward her. "Stand up."

She rose slowly. The last echo of daylight had vanished from the air, the moon alone now in the sky. It was night now, surely? "Come on," she whispered under her breath, the words repeating in her head, steady and urgent as the blows of the shovel. Come on, come on—

"Walk over to the grave."

Anna went, step by unsteady step. The brush of her clothing on her skin was overwhelming, stems and leaves crunching against her boots. Her ears rang. The hole grew in the dim lamplight, a sliver of yellow spilling down one rough wall, spackled shadows cast on the ground. Dark liquid spattered the mound of dirt, shining on the leaves. She looked at the open grave and knew suddenly that she was going to die here; she'd bargained, taken her chance. And now she was going to die, and there was nothing she could do about it.

"Turn around."

The men were looking at her, their faces pale in the gloom. Masks at a funeral.

"There was gold." Her voice sounded ragged in her ears. "You said you'd let me go if there was gold. How's this square?"

"Maybe the kid took you. Maybe you made… eyes at him. Saw your chance. Thought you could… get one over on us."

"I can settle you," she said, fast. She felt as it she were floating out of her body, watching herself talk. Like she'd passed through terror and into calm, still waters on the other side. "You said—"

Something in his face moved for the first time, coiling under the skin. ""Settle… me?" Blackbone said. His eyes were pinpricks in the darkness under his hat. Black as shotgun barrels drinking the world. "Is that what you think I am, conjure woman? A ghost? There's no… settling me. And you'll never get the chance to try."

The gloved hands worked the lever and raised the rifle.

A gun cracked out on the slope. Up on the ledge, Josiah made a high keening noise and plummeted over the edge, smacking into the dirt. The pistol went off, blasting a chunk of granite into stinging dust. Anna ducked at the sound and a blast of thunder punched her ears from the rifle, the air splitting over her head. Then she was diving forward and everything was chaos.

Muzzles flashed from among the stumps. Bullets hissed and pinged off the rock shelves. Somewhere horses screamed. The ringing in her ears pulsed, drowning all of it out. She hauled herself along the ground, breath sobbing in her throat, the trampled weeds scratching her face. Out of the corner of her eye she caught a glimpse of Blackbone whirling, buttons glinting in the lamplight, sprinting toward the end of the granite wall. The other men scattered for their weapons.

"We got you surrounded!" a voice shouted at the edge of hearing. "Give yourselves up!"

"Jesus Chrissst it hurts—"

No time to think. The gunshots were a wall of percussive sound, smashing against her ears, deafening. She grabbed the pistol out of Josiah's unresisting hand, fumbled the unfamiliar weight. She rolled on her back in time to see shadows scattering in the lamplight; Blackbone sweeping back toward her in a blur of blue-grey cloth, a sack in one hand, rifle in the other, moving low and fast toward the gold bars stacked by the grave.

"No you don't!" Rainey's voice was a muffled screech. He drew a pistol and fired, his shot cutting the cavalry hat off Blackbone's head. "Lay hands on me, will you? I'm settling with y—"

Blackbone swirled the rifle in his hand, tucked the butt under his arm and blew Rainey's stomach away. Even as the body fell he was moving again, face set.

"You're pinned! Give it up, goddammit!"

There was a rumbling under Anna's back, like a hornet's nest, buzzing and angry. Her ears rang. Blackbone crouched over the gold, shoving bars in the sack, and rose in a half crouch. Even now, she thought. Even now, he's never going to stop, and then he'll come for me—

She leveled the pistol at Blackbone and fired. The gun bucked in her hands; Blackbone jolted back, as if something had grabbed his shoulder. She had a brief glimpse of something dark staining his coat. Then he was working the lever action, spinning on her—

Something rose behind him, pale in the lamplight. Long arms bound in heavy wet links wrapped around his neck, hands twining inside the greatcoat. Huge eyes stared down from a head that rippled, maggot-white, rippled between dog and man and ox, all of them at once. She saw his head snap up, gloved hand straining for the thing's face. Fingers digging deep into the soft flesh. His flat eyes found hers, glittering cold as the stars.

A voice hissed like a knife through the gunfire and ringing in Anna's ears: *Wrong one…*

And then the pale thing fell backward, links wrapping around the outlaw's body, pulling him down into the grave, pulling the sack with him, the dirt crumbling under the remaining bars, spilling them all into the dark.

The pistol fell from her fingers. She lay back, gasping. The distant rumble of guns cut out a moment later, one last shot cracking down from overhead, scoring into the dirt. Up on the rock ledge, figures were moving in the trees. "Anyone moves again and I swear by God I'll shoot you," someone bawled from overhead. "I'll shoot you and save the judge the time. Guns *down!*"

***

"Well," Sheriff Martin Starks said, "It's a mess down here, for sure. Our own personal damn San Juan Hill."

Lanterns glowed on the graves, throwing out intersecting circles of yellow light, outlining the blood spatters on the trampled weeds. Two men were wrapping up the earthly remains of Montague Giacomo and some unnamed man with a broken nose. Luke Pataki and one Josiah Clint sat under a deputy's watchful gaze, their hands bound, the latter with a bandaged shoulder and a rag in his teeth for the pain. The rest of the posse were smoking, cigarettes glowing coal-red in the dark. Two bloodhounds panted at their feet.

"Landon Burwell got shot through the thigh," Joe said. "So we'll have to put him on one of the horses when we head back. Maynard and Damron got flesh wounds. And William Tiller's dead. Shot in the neck, bled out. They just found him up on the slope."

"Christ," Starks said. "Died a hero, at least. That's what his wife hears, Joe. Died in pursuit of notorious outlaws holding a young lady."

Joe nodded, solemn. "You want to go talk to her now? She didn't say much to me."

"Well, Joe," Starks said, accepting the satchel and walking stick, "you ain't personable like I am. Tell everyone we'll be ready to go soon."

He tucked the bag and stick under one arm and tramped over to where the girl sat against the rock ledge, where he tossed them down in front of her. She snatched them up quickly, hugging them to her chest. Her face was dirty under her hat, spattered in flecks of blood, eyes like a hunted animal's. Her hands shook a little in the lampglow. Nerves. Starks had seen it; folks holding tight during some trouble, going to pieces afterward.

"Well ma'am," he said, crouching in front of her. "I'm sorry it took us so long. We got just a little turned around out there, what with all that backtracking and creek-walking. But your things were a great help to us. Anna O'Brien, right?"

She looked at him and shook her head, her brow crinkling.

"You were a great help to us," Starks said again, louder. "What's the matter, girl? You a mute?"

"Can't hear," she said, just as loud. Tapped her ear, wincing.

"Oh, that'll wear off tomorrow," Starks said. "My name's Sheriff Starks, from Bakersmont. You're lucky, ma'am. There's not many that run with these types who can count their fingers after. They're killers."

"I wasn't—running with them."

Starks scratched his mustache. "Yeah, that's what these boys said. Told us you promised them gold out here to save your skin, then ran off with the washboy from the bank, and they found it when they tracked you.

Said you got within' a hair's breadth of getting yourself shot. One of them was surprised to hear you wasn't shot, and expressed a strong desire to do so himself. That's what I mean by you being lucky, ma'am. You happen to see what happened to Jack Diggs?"

She stared off, her eyes glassy. "Jack Diggs?"

"Blackbone Jack," Starks said. "He ain't here, as you can see. Though the two over there swear up and down he brought them here. Deputy Bobby says he saw a man in a greatcoat get shot, go down into the grave. Said there was something real queer about it. You see anything like that?"

"He went in the grave," Anna said. "Saw that."

"It's just that we checked, ma'am. He wasn't there."

Her face jerked up toward him, the motion sharp, and Starks found himself staring into a pair of sharp grey eyes, intent and serious. "No Blackbone?"

"No body," Starks said. "Just the Herriman kid and the coffin. Could be he got away in the shooting though I'll be damned if I know how. You heard the stories about him? Man's like a damn insect. Well, we'll get him eventually, or someone will. Man like that can't run forever. You see that gold they were talking about?"

Her back shuddered and she laughed, hollow in her throat. "I saw it."

"You see what happened to it?"

"Blackbone had it."

"And Blackbone's gone. And the gold's gone."

"Yeah." Anna's laugh shuddered out in her throat. Suddenly she was shaking all over, drawing her knees up to her chest. "Yeah," she said, through chattering teeth. "I—"

Starks rocked back on his heels a little, feeling awkward. "Ma'am... you ok?"

"Sheriff," she said, her voice strained. "I been hit, thrown down, grabbed by outlaws, had more guns in my face in two days than—-

Her hands squeezed her legs. Then she shoved herself to her feet, leaning on the walking stick, slinging the satchel over her shoulder. Her chest moved in deep breaths, her eyes closed for a moment as she got a grip on herself. When they opened she stuck her chin out. Pointed a nearly-steady hand at the grave. "You mind if I go over there?"

"I guess you can," Starks said.

He hooked his thumbs in his belt and watched her walk over, rummaging in her coat until she pulled out a pouch. She stared down at the hole for a moment, cocking her head like someone was talking to her. Then she thumbed the pouch open and dumped its contents out in a spray of white, scattering it over the grave. Shook it till it was empty, muttered something under her breath, and then tossed it down in there. Then turned around and came back.

Starks eyed her. "What was that?"

"Salt," Anna said, her jaw set. "All my salt. And if that doesn't work, nothing will."

"Ma'am—" Starks paused, chose his words carefully. "You want to come back to Bakersmont? You look like you been living rough a while. We can find someone to put you up for a night or two. Check you over."

"No," Anna said. "I'd like to go."

"Where?"

"Somewhere there's trees," Anna said. "And anywhere that ain't here."

WHERE WOODS HAVE NEVER KNOWN THE AXE

1903

You can joke," Big Henry said. "But there's things in this life Mr. Darwin's never considered, things your preachers never dreamed. I say so 'cause I've seen it, and I'll lay out any that disputes me."

Nobody did. He leaned forward toward the fire, staring at them all with sunken eyes. The men on the log opposite shifted under his gaze, their grins going crooked, uncertain. Above them the old-growth trees rose into the night, the firelight painting their boles, and sparks danced up in whirling motes to join the scattered stars. They sat and waited, and Anna O'Brien waited too.

She'd come to the logging camp while passing through, fading out of the night to join the rough men at the fire. They were brewing coffee and offered her some, and a seat on a newly-sawed chunk of wood. She warmed her hands and listened as they spoke of the day's business, of whether the hissing, spluttering steam saw would work, or if it would be better to cut the trunks by hand.

At first they watched their language. But the flask came out and made the rounds, and the younger men began telling of dangers and bloody injuries, keeping half an eye always on the rawboned woman sitting silent by the fire. Mangled limbs and accidents, first. Then rumors spread by the drunk and lily-livered; old Hide-Behind, who crept after you from trunk to trunk, ever at your back, so that you never saw him until it was too late; or the devil catamounts, the howling wampus cats that snuck into camps and left only bloody bedrolls behind them.

She turned her head away at the last, mouth tightening. The men read her expression as fear and laughed, drumming their feet and hooting. All but Big Henry, sitting at the other end of the fire. When he shifted and spoke, his low voice rumbled like a steam saw, cutting the conversation off.

"You don't know me, girl," he said now, his big shovel hands grasping his tin cup. His pocked bald head gleamed in the firelight. "Some of you boys, you don't know me well. But I been twenty years with an axe in my hand, and ten of them with the company in one part or another. I got a nose for the good groves, an eye for how to get 'em, how to ship 'em out. Five years back, the company put me on a good salary, set me to walking tracts they wanted to buy, see what I thought they could make out of it. I walked all over these mountains, boys, saw some queer things before I quit. But there's one I'll always recollect."

Someone put a log in the fire. Wood snapped and hissed, sparks racing up into the dark.

"The company had bought a big parcel sight-unseen, deep down in the Virginia country, as far west as that state goes. They sent a man out 'fore me, a local, but he took his money and run off, didn't come back. That's what they thought back East. So they sent me. It was hard country. I scrambled, boys, hand over hand sometimes, up ridgetops sharp and mean. Then I come up the last one and see it stretched out ahead: black valleys of chestnut and ash, king trees, all of 'em, poking their crowns through the mist. Good timber. But I didn't like it. Something in the shape of them stirred me wrong.

"Still, I's being paid, and paid well, so I went down in there, into the dark. I been to wood and forest and deep mountain cove, but nowhere I ever seen a place like that. Down there the sun don't show his face, and the branches stretch out thick and tangled, and the roots are knobby as old men's knees. The ground's deep in dead leaves and grey ivy. There's white flowers that come up like mushrooms, mushrooms that spread out like carpets. And a mist rolling overhead like a waiting thing.

"I walked it two days, blazing trees behind me, 'for I had a sense of them pressing in around me, pressing tight and hungry. The third day I thought I'd seen enough and I'd go report back. But I missed the blazes I'd set somehow. The trunks stretched out every way I looked, and the flowers swayed to follow me. I never been turned around in a forest before, boys, but I was turned around in that one, turned right around. But I had my compass and gun, and an ax for firewood, and I never minded living rough. Reckoned I'd shoot my supper and walk till I found my way out. Only—if there were game in those woods, I never saw it. No birds, no squirrels, not a racoon or possum. Just sounds at night, things slipping and scrabbling, and the flapping of wings in the dark. I ran out of food the fifth day, was hungry the sixth. Then on the seventh day, I come across a track up a hillside, a kept track, and I followed to see what was up the other end.

"I went up figuring on a cabin in a clearing, maybe a few cabins, maybe a garden and some homebrew and a daughter to dimple at. Some handy folk cutting out a life. I walked past steep mounds, all covered in mushrooms and white flowers, till I come to the foot of a cliff. Well, weren't no clearing, boys, no garden neither. But there was a cabin, laid right up at the edge of the rocks, under trees all cobbed over in ivy. The ivy climbed all over that cabin, too, growing up empty windows. I looked inside and saw a dirt floor covered in leaves, ivy growing over a table and green plates and puddling over lumps in the corners. I didn't like the look of that place, boys, not at all. But there were sounds out there in the forest, scrabbling and hissing, and night was coming on, blacker than black. I gathered up some firewood and went inside."

He took a sip from his tin cup, swallowed, and set it down. He was silent a moment, his eyes distant. Then he went on.

"I sat with my back to the little fire, looking at the room. I kept looking at that table and at the chairs, all thick-bundled in leaves, but for one that stood open and clear. I thought to go sit in it, get off the soft, wet floor. But something stopped me. I watched that table, and the table watched me back, and the fire got low behind me. I can't rightly describe what happened next. But as the fire got lower it's like I could see the room clearer, and it weren't the room I was in. It was a clean new cabin room with people gathered round the table for supper. Young people done up in old clothing, old like the first white men who came to the hills. They were sitting there all cold and quiet, gathered around that empty chair. Just eating, and watching it like I'd been."

"Sounds like a dumb supper," one of the men said, quiet. "Ever heard of that, Henry? This girl here, I guess she been to one or two in her time."

"Was asked once," Anna said, "before I was married. Never went."

"What's this, now?" Big Henry said.

"It's when a bunch of girls get together to see who they'll wed," the man said. "They cook a meal and set a table, all quiet, walking backwards, and leave an empty place for whoever shows. One of 'em might see a spirit of the man she's bound for in that chair. Sometimes a man get wind of it, comes knocking and sits down to hint at his sweetheart. It's an old custom, but I never saw harm in it."

"Old," Big Henry said slowly. "Yes, it's old, and these people were from an old time. But it weren't a dumb supper they was having. I sat there by a cold fireplace, on a clean floor, watching them eat as the room got clearer. Clear enough I could see they looked sick, pale and twisted like they'd had the ague. Clear enough I could see what they were eating, too. I guess I made a noise when I saw that, because all of them turned to look at me. They beckoned me, silent, pointed at that big empty chair. Wanting me to fill it. That chair pulled at me, boys, pulled me like a hole in the world, like the only thing could set it right was me sitting. Pulled me right up to my feet and toward the table. I was almost there when something snapped under my foot.

"Now, I've worked long enough to know snapping wood in I hear it. And I know the other sound, too. I looked down and saw something white under my feet, white and shiny. And then I saw that there were other bones on the floor, bones and clothing, years and years of clothing under the leaves. The thing on the table started beating like a heart, and drops pattered down from the roof, hot and stinging, like something big up there had a watering mouth. And the people at the table weren't people anymore.

They were bones too, old bones bound up in ivy and white flowers, mushrooms coming out of their eyes. They got up and came toward me, reaching out like they meant to shove me into that chair.

"Well, boys, I didn't wait around. I buried my axe in one of them and tore out of there, past the mounds, and I saw as I ran that each of them was a cabin swallowed up, and to this day I shudder at what stirred inside. You say a dumb supper's for calling sweethearts? Well they called something; or maybe something was waiting for the people who tried to settle that place, waiting to be called. Something that got down inside them and keeps them still. That's my story, and I'll drop the man that says I dreamt it."

One of the men gave a whistle, long and low. "Jesus, Henry."

"What did you tell the company?" Anna said.

Big Henry shrugged. "I told them there's good timber there, but hard to get at. Too hard to get at for now, since there's still easier groves to cut. But they own that land, own it on paper, and one day they'll get around to it. Maybe the steam-saw's enough for it, or fire. But I tell you boys, I'll never go back that way, not for all the money in the world. They can buy and sell that land from a hundred miles away, carve it up on a map, call it logged with the flick of a pen. I hope they don't. A wood that's never known the axe has known other things, older and meaner things. Let them stay there."

The fire popped and spluttered as they thought about that. The doomed trees loomed overhead, their branches whispering together against the sky.

PRETTY FLOWERS ARE MADE FOR BLOOMING

1903

W**hen the first fat drops fell on the dirt track**, Anna O'Brien said an unkind word and quickened her pace through the meadow.

Spring in the Carolina mountains was tilting into summer, and heavy clouds gathered along the ridgelines, the afternoon rains dropping in sudden, drenching curtains that turned the forests into a watercolor smear. Anna was heartily sick of it. Sick of the air that draped over everything like a heavy blanket, sick of soaked clothes, sick of her chafing wooden leg.

That was why—when she saw the cabin tucked back at the meadow's edge, sloping and rough-shingled in the grey light—she did the unmannerly thing by going up onto the porch and knocking sharply on the door. She was neither surprised nor offended when the woman who opened it held a gun.

"Ma'am," Anna said. Opening her hand, she stepped backward to the edge of the porch. Behind her the rain let loose, hammering down into the grass.

The woman's eyebrows rose. She was some years older than Anna, and rangy, with a dress of much-patched calico and frizzy copper hair. The rifle barrel bobbled for a moment before she brought it to her side, not pointing it at Anna but not pointing it away either. "Who're you?"

"Anna O'Brien, ma'am. Just a traveler."

Beyond the sloping porch the rain thickened, the treeline melting away, sheets of water pouring over the lip of the roof. The woman scrutinized Anna, taking in her soaked shirt and sodden coat and the way her big hat drooped over her grey eyes. The rifle dropped a bit more. "Cora," she said. "What's it you want?"

"A drought would be pretty nice."

Cora's lip twitched. "You looking for a place to dry off? That it?"

Anna's voice came out in a rush. "If it's trouble, I'll take a barn, a shed—"

A voice called out from inside, musical and questioning. Cora tensed at the sound of it, looking back over her shoulder so that the cords stood out in her neck. When she looked back she chewed her lip, thinking it over; then the suspicion that had flickered up in her weather-beaten face just as quickly flickered out. "We got neither," she said. "I guess you better come inside. We're fixing supper."

The front room was cramped and dim, with a scuffed wedding quilt hanging on one wall and balls of crumpled newspaper stuffed around the window frames. In the center of the room stood a hand-carved table; in the back corner was a washbasin and an iron stove, bordered on either side by shelves laden with bouquets of wilting flowers. Pink and red petals drooped like tongues.

A small woman sat beside the stove, her dark hair hanging loose, long tapering fingers peeling potatoes and throwing pieces in an iron skillet. She rose from her stool as Cora let Anna in, her back and shoulders taut as a bowstring. "Who's this?"

"Says her name's Anna." Cora latched the door and leaned the rifle against the nearest wall. "She needs a place to dry off, Maggie. It's bucketing down again."

The reserve in the other woman's face flowed away, replaced by a broad, warm smile. She had a pretty, lively face, her brown eyes showing the first scattering of crows feet. Setting the skillet down, she came over to take Anna's bags and walking stick. "I'm Margaret. Good to know you, Anna. Cora, would you mind the stove? I'll take her on back and get her settled, see if we got something that fits."

Anna opened her mouth to say that she could settle herself, but Margaret closed a hand on her wrist and swept her into the blue darkness of the back bedroom. The small woman moved now with brisk efficiency, her lively face screwing up in concentration as she rummaged through the closet. She pulled out a towel and a blue dress, dropped them on the bed beside Anna, and turned her back, her hand outstretched behind her. "Go ahead and pass me your wet things," she said. "I'll get them hung up."

Anna peeled her way out of her boots and clothes, sweat and stale rainwater running down her shoulders and curling her hair. She darted over, left leg clumping, to drop them in Margaret's hand.

"You've got a loud step," Margaret said, keeping her back turned. "Go ahead and get dry. Come on out when you're ready."

"Thanks."

She sat there a moment after Margaret swept out, collecting herself, taking in the smell and sounds of the place; the murmur of conversation beyond the door, the smell of lard and frying potatoes, and the endless patter of rain on the roof. After a moment, she dried herself and undid the straps on her wooden left leg, sliding it off and toweling the stump, before clutching the straps in both hands and breathing warmth into them. Once the headache stilled, she shrugged on the dress, buckled her leg back into place, and walked back out into the light of the front room.

The two women glanced over as she entered, Cora hanging Anna's wet clothing on a line above the stove, Margaret standing alongside, her hand already sliding away from the taller woman's back. A wave of dislocation swept against Anna as their eyes fell on her. She was desperately aware of the thinness of the cloth, of how long it had been since she'd worn a dress, of the rough oak approximation of her shin and foot. There would be questions now, questions she didn't care to answer, and she steeled herself for them, feeling more naked than she'd ever felt bathing in the woods.

"You clean up very nice," Margaret said.

Beside her Cora eyed Anna, made a soft hmp in her throat, and stirred the potatoes. "You put her in my dress?"

"Oh, you're both skin and bones," Margaret said. "Come on, sit down. Supper's hot."

Anna swallowed, took a breath, and came over. The knocking of her foot on the boards sounded loud to her, and she looked at the table for something to say. There were four place settings there, three of them full. The fourth stood empty at the foot of the table, without a chair to accompany it. "We waiting for somebody?"

A cloud passed over Margaret's face. "Pay it no mind," she said. "We just like to be ready, that's all. Just like to keep a place out for whoever shows. Cora, would you say grace?"

Together they tucked into fried potatoes and cornbread and leftover stew, listening to the sound of the rain pounding down. It had been weeks since Anna's last hot meal, and she bolted it down, the light spices nearly overpowering after a diet of bread and cold jerky. She was mopping up the grease with a bit of cornbread when she looked up to see the women staring at her, their own food forgotten on the table.

"My lord," Cora said.

Margaret leaned forward, fascinated. "I swear that plate was full a moment ago. "

"Sorry." Anna ducked her head. "It's just...it's good."

"I'm glad you think so," Margaret said, her voice arch. Beside her, Cora's eyes rolled. "So where you traveling to, Anna? Visiting family?"

"Just walking," Anna said. "Seeing the country."

"And how's it?" Cora said.

"Wet," Anna said. She looked down at the plate, closed her eyes a moment, pushing down the fluttering in her chest. It occurred to her that she should say more, keep talking. "Sorry," she said again. "It's wet. I was out west of here, saw flooding near the timber-tracts. Water tore up a mill while I was passing through. Washed out some bridges. Nearly washed out me—"

They talked a while about the timber business, about the great properties and the logging camps springing up everywhere, more every year, and the old groves being felled and rolled down into the flatland rivers or run down on the railroads. It was a trade, they all agreed, though

Anna remarked of coming across hillsides stripped bare of everything but stumps, the graveyards of old forest standing open and scarred against the green of the surrounding mountains. How was a family supposed to make a living in a place like that, where the hogs couldn't run and the ramps wouldn't grow? It was dangerous work, too. Margaret's husband had worked the timber until a rolling log took him and two others, she told Anna, her voice displaying little in the way of emotion; she'd been in desperate straits until Cora came up from Franklin to help out.

Anna stumbled there again, thinking about Margaret's hand on Cora's side and unsure of what that meant. How long had she been helping out? She had an intimation of something slightly beyond her, something she didn't know how to put into words. It was in the careful, slightly distant politeness with which they guided her away from asking more about their past. And there was something else, a bit sharper, in the way their eyes slid over the table every now and again to rest on that empty plate, and just as quickly slid away.

But it was easy to talk to Margaret. Cora set some coffee on the stove and lit the kerosene lamps, making the cramped room cozy. It grew cozier when Margaret served them coffee, complete with a dollop of homebrew to give it warmth; cozier still when Cora fetched out a mandolin from the back room and Margaret sang, "Pretty Saro" and "O' the Cuckoo," in a high sharp voice as Anna kept time on the tabletop.

"You know," Margaret said, when Cora set the instrument down and took a sip of her coffee, "you gave us a start, knocking on the door like that. You ought to shout before you come up on someone's property."

"I know it," Anna said. "I just got so tired of being wet."

"I don't normally greet folks that way," Cora said. "I thought you were—"

Margaret shook her head, a quick little shake. And because Anna'd had a bigger dollop of whiskey than she was used to, she said, "So who are we really waiting for?"

Brawley, said the patter of the rain on the roof, droplets bouncing on wood and running together, gurgling and chuckling down the windows. *Brawley.*

"Nobody," Margaret said. Her expressive face had clamped back down, the way it had been when Anna first came into the house, and beside her Cora's eyes went cold. "Well— somebody. He's been coming around these last few months. We've had some trouble."

"The kind makes you open the door with a gun?"

"Worse." Cora's rough face was flint sharp in the lantern-light. "You say you've traveled some? Ever heard bad stories? Witch stories?"

"Some," Anna said.

"Those… stories you heard," Margaret said, her voice halting now. "They're true about him."

"Well ran dry." Cora glared at Anna, defiant, as if waiting for her to smile, to say they were overreacting. "We thought, ok, sometimes that happens. But then it went wet again, and what we pulled up in it, we couldn't drink. Our milk turned. Our egg yolks come out black, squirming. And there's something else that comes, sometimes. At night. Comes prowling around and around, out in the dark."

"He wasn't so bad at first," Margaret said quietly. "Came around with flowers for us. For me. But now—"

Brawley, sighed the flowers, in their piles on the shelves. *Brawley*…

The rain on the roof shifted, the sound wavering, ceasing, and then returning full force. Wood creaked on the porch, the floorboards near the door bowing as if under great weight. Margaret's face went ashen. Cora's chair scraped back, her eyes fixing on the gun leaning against the wall. She had barely taken a step when the latch clicked up and the door swung open, revealing the smiling, narrow face of a man.

He stood with his legs spread and thumbs hooked in his suspenders, a thin young man with a scraggly beard and a dry coat hooked carelessly on his shoulders. His sharp lips lifted, the kind of smile that hinted its owner knew great secrets and wanted everyone to know it. Yellow lamp light pressed against his front, filtering past him and onto the gloom of the porch. Something huge and shaggy stirred out there, just beyond the light; something breathed a deep, wet breath, like a hog with its nose in a carcass. The floorboards groaned. Eyes shone for a moment, horribly knowing. Then it was gone into the night, leaving only the rain and the man standing at the threshold.

"Brawley Gabal," Cora said, voice flat as a whetstone.

"Hello, Cora," said the man, striding three steps over to the table. The door shuddered itself shut behind him. A finger crooked lazily and the kitchen stool slid over to the foot of the table. He sat down on it without looking, crossing his leg and smiling his crooked smile at them all. "Hello, pretty Maggie. I see y'all been eating. Who's this?"

"Just a stranger come in out of the rain," Margaret said hurriedly. "We figured to feed her. But we left you a place too, Brawley, see, right there."

"I do see that." The man's gaze spidered over Anna, and she was horribly aware of the way the dress hung off her, of how far away her coat and pants were, hanging above the stove. His tongue darted out and touched his lips. Then his eyes were back on Maggie, intent as a cat. "I see Cora's got her mandolin out, too. When was the last time y'all pulled that out for me? Y'all been making friends?"

"Just being hospitable," Cora said.

Brawley flicked a hand over his hair, smoothing it down. "You know," he said, "I got a friend too. He's waiting outside. Y'all want to meet him? 'Cause if I come back and find my chair filled again, you will. Cora, would you serve me up?"

Stiffly, the tall woman took his plate and walked over to the stove, her arms brushing the bushels of dried flowers. Anna watched now, counting steps; four to the stove from the head of the table, where her clothing was drying and her rucksack and satchel leaned against the shelves. There was salt in there, and some silver coins. Could she get back to it without arousing suspicion? She saw Cora glance sidelong at the rifle leaned up by the door, the flint look in her eyes sharpened now to steel. Their eyes met.

Brawley flicked a hand and laid the batch of flowers that appeared there on the table. Petals of garish red settled on the wood. "I brought these for you, Maggie."

"They're lovely," Margaret said in a small voice.

"They are," Brawley agreed. Light flickered in the kerosene lamps. "You can put them with all the others."

Cora set his food down and hovered behind him, her eyes downcast. Brawley spooned up his food lazily, taking his time, like he wasn't savoring the taste so much as enjoying the way they all waited for him to finish. "This is good. You always cook good, Maggie. Sure better than I could."

"I'm surprised at that," Anna said.

Brawley's jaw worked over a mouthful of potatoes. "Why's that, little girl?"

"Seems you can make a house do what you like," Anna said. "Neat tricks like that, I guess they come in handy in the kitchen."

Brawley shrugged, disinterested, and his gaze went back to Maggie. But Anna took a gulp of coffee and set the pewter cup down sharply on the wooden table, so that his eyes cut back.

"That power," she said. "How'd you come by it? Your… friend?"

Brawley stopped chewing. His head came around, really looking at her now, his narrow face pinched in thought. "That's right," he said. "I caught him and broke him, and made him learn me in the secret ways. I don't guess you'd care for the finer details."

"Try me," Anna said. She felt Cora and Margaret's frowns, but kept her face on Brawley.

"I went up into the hill bogs to do it," Brawley said. "Brought me a bible and a fistful of rocks, threw them rocks at the sky and told God I wanted no part of him. I buried that bible in the muck and danced on it. When he came, I wrestled him down until he swore he'd serve." He looked at Anna to see her expression, and found nothing there. "What do you know about it?"

"Enough," Anna said.

"Why," he said, and his grin flashed across his face. "You got the power too, don't you? What'd you trade for it?"

"Nothing worth talking about."

"Come on, we're all friends here." Brawley scooted his stool forward. "Let's talk shop. Was it your leg? I seen that wooden thing you got under that dress. Did you get a good price for that? Flying, maybe?" His voice was oozing, sympathetic, like he had the measure of her now. He stretched, arms rising like a man delighted to wake up in the morning, bare feet coming up off the floor. "Now *me*, I did all right in my dealing."

"You traded something else," Anna said, eyes steady. "But if you don't miss it I guess it wasn't worth much."

Brawley's smile froze. "I don't think I like your manners."

"I know I don't like yours," Anna said. The whiskey and coffee sang inside her, burning out through her limbs. "You don't walk into someone's house uninvited and put your feet up. Didn't your mama ever teach you that?"

"Oh, that," Brawley said, and waved his hand as if at a fly. "We're old friends, Maggie and me. I known her since she was married. I come back and I find her living with her sister here, and I thought, that's no way for such a fine woman to live. So I been coming by to help out. Maggie, tell this lady how helpful I am."

Across the table, Margaret stared at both of them in mute horror. Cora stepped back, away from Brawley toward the door.

"You can scare them," Anna said. She took another sip of coffee, and deliberately set the cup down and slid it across the table. "But you and your friend don't scare me. I seen worse than you."

An ugly glint flashed in Brawley's eyes. "Ooh, Maggie. Your guest's got a mouth on her. Ain't I got a right to be here? You gonna let me sit here and be insulted? Well, fine. I'm running low on patience, Maggie, and I can't put the matter before us off any longer. What's it to be?"

Margaret opened her mouth, but Anna cut in, smooth, keeping Brawley's gaze. "You got some kind of claim on this woman?"

"Her heart," Brawley said. His hand flicked up to smooth down his hair, and his smile fanned back out across his face. "Her kind, soft heart. And what's between us ain't any concern of yours. Maggie, you know what I can give you. I've been coming round your door long enough for you to know. You got such *warmth* in you. Woman like you shouldn't be alone, with just your sister for company. Come with me and I'll soothe and comfort you all your long life. I want everything that beats inside you, down beneath your white breast." His voice was an ingratiating whine. "Please. Give me your heart."

Margaret's fingers trembled on the table. "Well?" Brawley hissed. His eyes were locked on her face, drinking her in, his expression desperate and hungry. Behind him movement flickered, a quick flurry of footsteps as Cora swept across the room, snatched up the rifle and brought it to her shoulder, aiming it at his head.

"Get out," she said, thumbing back the safety. "Or I swear to god I'll shoot you."

"Maggie?" Brawley said.

Maggie's breath shuddered out. She looked up at him, her hand clenched. "No. That's your answer, Brawley Gabal. I'm sorry, but no. Please don't come back."

A flicker of hurt swept across the man's face, followed by something that looked to Anna like fear. A red flush rose up in his gaunt cheeks, his lips pulling back to bare his teeth. Slowly he stood and raised his hands. "I'm sorry," he said. "I guess I been too flowery. That's my problem. Too much a poet. I'll be direct."

His arms jerked.

The lamps went out, darkness dropping sudden and hard on them all. The gun went off and something shattered on the other side of the cabin. Then the frame shook, wood splintering, wind howling inside the front room, lashing Anna's face. Something huge moved over the boards, bowling her over and crumpling her to the floor. She struggled up, heard the crack of furniture against the walls, a shrill scream. For a split second the snuffling sound passed Anna, a blast of rank skunk-odor that made her retch, the wind tugging at her dress. Then there was only silence, and the dark.

The lamps reignited. Anna lay there a moment, dazed, staring at the scattered chairs and overturned table, the wedding quilt crumpled in the corner, splashes of spilled coffee black on the wooden floor. Broken shelving lay amid drifts of dried flowers. Wet air rolled over her. As she staggered up, leaning against the wall for support, she saw the door hanging off its hinge, the frame bowed out from some great impact.

A small, dark haired form huddled on the other side of the room, hands clasped over her head. "Is it over?"

"He's gone," Anna said.

Margaret sat up, put a hand to her forehead and drew it back bloody. She looked at her palm, and then up at Anna with wide, white eyes. "Where's Cora?"

Spatters of rain dripped from the wreckage of the door frame. On the floorboards the coffee dregs quivered and flowed, shaping out dark, splotching letters.

Giv me yur heart
Hanging tree
By dawn
or sister dies

Margaret shook her head, her face stunned. And then the stunned look crumpled and she curled over on the floor, reaching toward the letters. She wiped at them with her hand, scrubbed at them, beat at the floorboards in a sudden flurry of motion, a sob tearing out of her throat. The letters stayed. Not until she laid her head down on the boards and wept did they finally sink away through the cracks. That, more than anything, told Anna everything she needed to know about Brawley Gabal.

The rain-patter dwindled outside, clammy air curling through the house through the wreckage of the door. Anna squared her shoulders and went to kneel beside Margaret, slipping a hand on her shoulder. "We're going to get her back. I promise."

Margaret sobbed again, her hands twisting themselves up in her dress.

"Maggie?"

"Don't you call me that," Margaret said, shoving Anna away. Her eyes appeared through the curtain of her dark hair, red and angry. "Don't you dare. That's for Cora. Oh Jesus, he took Cora, he took Cora and it's your fault, we should never have let you in, why couldn't you just keep *quiet*—"

"Margaret, listen—"

"Listen to you!" Margaret snarled. "He took Cora 'cause of you! You couldn't stop *pushing* him, like you knew anything about him, like you knew what he could do—"

"*Listen.* You don't know witchery, Margaret, that's not your fault. Nobody should have to know. But you know men, don't you? You think this is 'cause I pushed him? You think there was a way you could have told him no he'd have heard? When would you have liked to have tried? After he stole you away? Years after? It was always gonna come to this. Him pushing you." She reached out again, her voice soft. "You know that."

"He told me he wanted my heart when he gave me the first set of flowers," Margaret said. "I should've told him then. I should've… I should have… "

Anna studied her, face set and serious. "We aren't talking about love, are we?"

"No," Margaret said. "We're not. He wants my heart. He wants to pull it out of me, says without it I can live forever with him. And I have to do it. I can give it up, and he'll let her go." Her eyes glittered with tears. "If I don't, he'll kill her and then he'll just come here and take it—"

"He wants you scared, not thinking straight." Anna took her arm. "*Think.* He could have stolen you, plucked your heart out. But he didn't. He took Cora. He can't take it from you; he needs you to *give* it to him. That's why he's been after you so hard and so long. He's trying to lean on you, make you do what he wants. And that doesn't have to work."

Margaret sniffed in a deep breath, put her hands over her eyes, and exhaled. "But what can we do?"

"You don't know witchery," Anna said. "I do. You know what the hanging tree is? How to get there?"

Margaret nodded.

"Good," Anna said. "Go get the gun and any bullets Cora had. And turn around. I'm going to get dressed."

She shucked the dress off in the far corner and wiggled into her pants and shirt, the fabric still damp and cool against her skin. Her hat settled with a comforting weight on her head. Shrugging on her coat and satchel, she thumbed through bundles of medicinal plants until she found what she was looking for: a pouch of salt. She weighed it in her palm a moment, lips pursed. Salt was good for hags and haints, and sometimes good for spirits; would it be good for Brawley? She'd never seen anyone move things about like that, crooking their finger and making the house dance to their tune. Could he do that anywhere, with anything? Or was there something about the house—

Her gaze slid over to the broken shelving and the clutter of flowers.

"Margaret, are all of those from Brawley?"

"All of them." Margaret stuffed a fistful of bullets into the pocket of her apron, picked up the rifle, and checked it. A white shawl half-hung off her shoulders, and she tugged it up in a distracted motion. "He always brought flowers. Why?"

"I wonder," Anna said. "I don't like having anything he gave you in the house. We better take them with us."

Margaret fetched out a sack and broom and together they scooped up the flowers, the stalks brittle and sharp against their hands. Three times Anna swept the floor, gathering loose petals, as Margaret glanced more and more often at the dark ruin of her door. Finally Anna tied the sack and passed it to Margaret, who hefted it on her shoulder.

"All right," she said. "Let's go get her."

Clammy air swirled around them as they stepped out into the night, sticky with the smell of wet mulch and wood. A fine misting drizzle beaded the surface of their clothes. Margaret set off across the field, walking fast, Anna keeping up as best she could. Fireflies flickered like ghostlights beyond the faint amber glow of the kerosene lanterns, the night thick and pressing in, shrinking their world to a small circle of illuminated grass. Then the grass gave way and tree trunks loomed up before them, a ruined wall with cracks of impenetrable shadow that swallowed them up.

They found themselves on a narrow path beneath the black trees. Margaret kept moving, winding her way along a game trail that pressed through clumps of snaring witch-hobble and rhododendron. Three times Margaret led them up forks in the path. Their lantern glow bobbed through the black, the light bouncing over logs, on carpets of beaded moss and bulbous white mushrooms, spangling on the rivulets and puddles that wound across the rocky trail. Wet leaves slapped Anna's face, spattering her shirt. From everywhere came the dripping of water and the piping of tree frogs, blending into a blanket of sound that made Anna's breath sound loud and harsh to her own ears.

"Anna?" Margaret's voice was a soft whisper. Her lantern creaked as it swung, making her shadow dance. "We'll be there soon. What are we going to do?"

"You'll see," said Anna, who wasn't sure yet. "Why did you tell him you were sisters?"

Margaret's head turned over her shoulder, her face pale from behind the cloud of her wet hair. She clambered up over a shelf of rock, and reached out a hand to help Anna up. "I didn't."

"Oh," Anna said. "I didn't… think you were."

"What do you think we are, Anna O'Brien?" Margaret shot her look from under lowered brows.

"Friends?"

The noise Margaret made in her throat was very like Cora's. She flicked away a strand of Anna's hair and patted her on the shoulder, her touch motherly. Then she shook her head, turned and set off again. Anna hurried up behind her, feeling like something clumsy and dull that had blundered into a place of fine pottery, wrecking and stomping. Heat rushed up into her cheeks. "I been married, you know," she said, more loudly than she intended.

"Ain't we all." A smile ghosted across Margaret's lips. "Still—you hear that?"

They pressed together on the narrow trail, lanterns raised high. Anna listened hard, trying to ignore the rustle of wet branches and the soft echoes of dripping rainwater. Out in the dark the frogs had gone silent. The fireflies flashed and blinked like stars.

Beside her Margaret swallowed. "I heard… "

Anna put a finger to her lips.

Somewhere back behind them a branch snapped in the dark. Slowly, Margaret set her lantern down. She loaded the rifle and brought it up to her shoulder, sighting down the barrel in the direction they'd come. Her shoulders rose in a steadying breath, and her face twisted in disgust. Anna smelled it too: a pungent odor of sweat and skunk musk curling on the cool air, overpowering against the leaf mould. Coming up from downslope, against the wind.

"What is it?" Margaret's breath came fast in Anna's ear.

"Brawley's friend," Anna said. "Go up the trail and keep your lantern covered. Take the flowers. When you get to the clearing, hang back. I'll be along."

Margaret shot her a disbelieving look. "Don't you want the gun?" "Won't do me any good," Anna said, wishing she sounded more sure. Twigs crackled in the brush; far down the trail, a pair of green lights appeared, steady and growing. "Go on! I'll catch up."

Behind her, Margaret's footsteps hurried away, the darkness drawing ever closer as her lantern disappeared through the trees. Anna leaned on her walking stick, the lantern at her feet. The smell washed against her, harsh against her throat. Her hand dropped into the satchel.

The green lights grew into eyes, reflecting flat and featureless in the lamp glow. The rest of it took shape around them; a four-legged hill of fur and bone emerging slowly from the dark, heavy jaws hanging open, lips raised over curling fangs. Muscles moved like great ropes in its hide. It snarled as it approached, a deep, liquid sound that rolled around the trunks.

"Well?" Anna said.

The beast pressed closer. Saliva dripped from a yellowing tusk.

"Don't play this with me," Anna said. "I didn't get much of a look at you before, but now I'm sure. I don't think Brawley wrestled you down. Not if you didn't want to be wrestled."

The thing cocked its head like a man. Then it sat back on its haunches, tongue twitching in serpentine wriggles. "You guessed."

"That you were the brains?" Anna said. "Didn't take much. He ain't too bright, your Brawley. Thinks he can beat a hog of the bogs, or threaten his way to a woman's heart."

"I tried to tell him," the bog hog said mildly. Its voice was rich, marred only by the slavering popping of its lips. The long, forked tongue

slithered out and up, licking the side of its warty snout. "She took his flowers, so he's got some hold on her and hers, enough to work his will. But he could never go further. A fool. Still, he'll get me a heart."

Anna frowned and shifted against the walking stick. "What do you want it for?"

The bog hog grinned a dog-grin. "I have a hole inside me that only heart-meat can fill. Hers. His. It's all the same to me, so long as it's freely given. A closed heart just doesn't have the taste."

"Seems a strange way to treat a girl he's sweet on."

"Oh, Brawley made a *bargain*." The great belly waggled as it yawned and stretched. "Three months ago tonight, I lent him power and told him he owed me a heart. When the girl gives it to him, he'll cut it out on the hanging tree and speak the seven words I taught him, and then he'll raise her up and marry her and have her the rest of his long days. Perhaps he'll be happy."

Something in the creature's voice made Anna's eyes narrow. "What's he really gonna get?"

The bog hog smiled a horrible smile. "Bloody hands and a body, most likely. Can't say how much use either will be. He'll be angry, but there are so many other women. He can have as much power as he wants while he wins their hearts. He can try it again and again." It winked. "Maybe it'll work eventually."

"No," Anna said. "I'm putting a stop to it."

The bog hog threw back its head and barked, a hoarse eruption of amused sound. Its eyes turned appraising. "Is that right? He bade me make sure his Margaret gets there safe. Didn't say anything about you. A heart needs to be freely given, it's true. But I could about stomach the rest."

"Oh, you don't want me," Anna said, and pulled her hand out of the satchel. In it was a pouch, open and white in the lamplight. "I'm no good. I'm too… salty."

The bog hog sat very still.

"How does Margaret break the witchery?" Anna said. "The one he laid on her with the flowers."

"Why should I tell you?" hissed the bog hog. Its glowing eyes fixed on her hand.

"Because if you don't," Anna said, "I'll wrestle you, and I won't do it like Brawley did. No bible buried in muck and no rocks. No. I'll use this." Her fingers tipped, and a scattering of salt whispered against the sodden ground. "You want to try it?"

The bog hog's jaws snapped at her, the sound echoing like a gunshot. Its forefoot rose, five toes tipped with sharp trotters digging into the ground. But it came no closer. "What does it matter to you?"

"I could ask you the same," Anna said. "You lent Brawley power? That means you have a claim on him if he doesn't deliver. Don't you?"

All expression slipped from the bog hog's face. It considered her, its eyes shining cold and flat in the lantern-light, the tongue slipping back inside the great bony jaws. Then the smile came creeping back up over its long face. "You've got some nerve, don't you? I like that. Let's see what happens, then." It rose and shook itself, matted fur bristling. "Scatter the flowers at his feet, and three times forswear him. That will break his hold on her."

"Good," Anna said. "Reckon I can about handle it from there."

The bog hog's lips drew back one last time. It stepped back away from the lantern, until it was just a hulking shadow against the rainswept night. "Perhaps," whispered the voice. "Better get going. He's getting impatient."

Its glowing eyes faded, dwindling into the dark.

Anna stood there a moment longer, until she was sure she was alone. She clutched the pouch to her breast for two long breaths, her hand trembling, scattering grains of salt over her shirt. Then she slipped it into the satchel, picked up the lantern, and headed up the trail, moving as fast as she dared over the uneven ground.

Three turns of the path later she saw a faint glow up ahead, sickly and white through the thickets. She dropped her lantern down by her leg, approaching slow and careful over the mud. The trees thinned out, giving way to tangles of tall brush, and she kept behind them, peering out through gaps in the leaves.

Beyond the brushline the forest opened into a broad clearing broken by slabs of flat wet rock and drifts of grass and cranberry. A solitary elm tree stood in a bushy copse in the center of the stones, lamps floating in the air around the twisted trunk, spinning in slow circles a foot above the ground. Strange patterns of light rippled on the slabs. Two figures stood beneath the withered branches: a woman on her knees, her hair copper red, and a man pacing back and forth in front of her with quick, violent strides. A big hunting knife glimmered in his hand.

Anna considered the blade unhappily. There wasn't much chance of getting the drop on him, not with so much open space to cross; she could try circling around, keep the tree trunk between them, but the more she looked at it the less she liked the chances. Salt had worried the bog hog, and it might worry Brawley. But she didn't like to put a pouch of salt and a walking stick against a knife.

She was still thinking about it when something moved over to her side. Ferns rustled and a pale face peered up from behind an overgrown log, a smear of crusted blood black beneath wet hair. "Anna?"

"Here." She slipped over to the log, circling the bracken and kneeling down beside Margaret. Even in the gloom the other woman's knuckles shone white on the rifle stock. The smile she put on when she caught Anna looking was watery, and failed to cover the strain on her face; her eyes were wide and scared.

"I thought you might not come back," she said. "I thought to take a shot at him, but I don't dare, with him holding that knife so close to Cora. What happened?"

"Got some answers. Brawley witched y'all with the flowers he gave you. I reckon that's how he made things in the house move, messed up your well, walked in and out as he pleased. You have to give them back."

"Just...hand them to him?" Margaret's voice was bewildered. "That's it?"

"A bit more than that," Anna said. "You have to dump them at his feet, tell him you renounce him. You have to say it three times, or it won't work."

"And if it does work?"

Anna chewed her lip. "I reckon he won't be able to witch you two anymore, throw your things around like he did. But he'll still be a man with a knife. And he'll still want your heart." She tapped her thigh, fingers bouncing, waiting for inspiration. "I better come with you."

"No, you better not." Margaret's jaw set, and her hand closed tight on Anna's arm. "He's all keyed up. Me he expects, but God only knows what he'll do to Cora if he sees you. Please just… stay back."

She scooped up the sack of flowers and the rifle, slipped over the log, and walked determinedly toward the floating lamps, her head held high. For a moment she was backlit against the glow, a line of gold etched around her shape, and then she stepped through and the light washed over her mud-spattered shawl and apron, glinting dully off the gun. "Brawley," she called. Brawley stopped in his pacing as Margaret came into view, leaning back and cocking his head. Abruptly he was all smiles, his body arching in delight, teeth glinting white. "Why, you came!" he sang out, and bounded toward her. "Seeing sense all of a sudden. Look at that. That's what I like about you, Maggie. You see how things are."

Margaret stopped in a patch of grass a few paces away from the tree. "Cora? You alright?"

The kneeling woman looked up, her eyes glassy. When she saw Margaret she struggled for a moment, arms jerking, her body straining against some invisible force. Then she went slack again.

"She won't move till I let her." Brawley stuck his thumb in his suspenders and gestured with the knife, swaying with self-delight. "Come on, Margaret. We're gonna be so happy, you and me. We're gonna see the whole *world.* All the nations of the earth. Your sister won't be able to keep us apart anymore. Won't that be fine?" He peered closer at her. "Why, Maggie, you're bleeding."

"Brawley," Margaret said, voice shaking, "there's something I got to—"

Brawley came toward her, his footsteps crunching on the flaking rock. "How did you get cut up? Are you alright?"

"Brawley—"

His free hand reached out toward her face. All at once she swung the rifle up, putting the barrel between them. "Don't touch me," she snapped. "You want to know how I got cut up? You and your friend broke down our door, threw me against a wall." "Maggie, I had to make you see." Brawley grinned at her, like it was all a joke, like if he grinned long enough she'd see it and laugh. The gun's no use, Anna thought from her perch along the brushline. It's the flowers, she has to return the flowers, otherwise he'll just—

Brawley flicked a lazy finger down and the rifle twisted in Margaret's hand like a living thing. The chamber clicked and bullets spilled onto the grass. Then the gun tore itself out of her fingers and went skidding and bouncing along the stone. "You want your sister free? You know what you got to do. Just give me your heart. When I'm done you won't hardly miss it."

Wordlessly, Margaret swung the sack down off her shoulder, stepped up to Brawley and dumped the contents at his feet. Flowers piled out, petals fluttering and spinning in the air. Around them, the floating lamps shuddered. "Brawley Gabal," she said, looking him dead in the eye, "I renounce you." The lamps shook, whirling like tops. Brawley shook his head like he didn't understand what he was hearing. "Maggie—"

"*Don't call me that.* I renounce you!"

Brawley lips drew back from his teeth. "No!"

"I renou—"

His hand thrust out. The shawl on Margaret's shoulders wriggled and tore with a rip of fabric, twining around her lips and jerking her head back. Her legs kicked out, tearing furrows at in the grass as she clawed at the shawl. Brawley swayed for a moment, his eyes widening, and then he snarled and twisted his palm toward the ground, breathing hard, forcing her to her knees. "Trying to break my claim? Is that right? I got you fair and square, Maggie. You took the flowers! Trying to throw them back in my face? Well go on now! Try it!"

He kicked at her legs, buckling her to the stone. A vein throbbed in his gaunt cheek, sweat dripping down his forehead. "Don't want me? Well, fine. I got enough on you still to hold you, and I still got until dawn to win my friend a heart. I tried sweet, nobody can say I didn't. Now I'll cut and cut until one of you begs me to take it. Maybe—"

"Brawley Gabal," Anna said, and stepped out of the trees, her satchel on her shoulder, walking stick loose in her hand. She had a thought now, the barest bones of a plan. Salt against knife. Ten paces to find out if it would work. "A word?"

His face swung toward her, venomous with hatred. "You."

"Me." She nodded at him and came forward three steps, winding through coils of cranberry. Her hand dipped in the satchel. "You made a bad deal, Brawley. Lost even before you started. You've taken a woman captive, threatened another, made their lives a misery. Witching ain't illegal, Brawley, but abduction? You'll hang from that tree. If you're lucky."

Brawley hooted, stepping over Margaret's writhing body and pointing the knife at Anna. Seven steps. "You think the law can touch me? Come any closer and I'll use this knife. I'll do it, I swear on… on…"

Anna's eyes were shadowed beneath the hat. "Your heart?"

"No," Brawley whispered. "How did you—"

"Thing is," Anna said, and came forward again, stopping three strides from Brawley. She shrugged her satchel off, rolling her shoulders. "You still got some power over them. Not as much as you had, but some. But me? You got no claim over me. Come on now. Don't you want to see what I traded my leg for?"

Brawley paced forward and hesitated, two strides away now, the blade tracing patterns in the air. His shoes made rings in the shallow rock puddles. The lantern light spun and refracted on his clothes.

Anna dropped the walking stick by her side. She raised her hands, one fist held back and clenched, the other open. The fingers on her open hand twisted into an arcane pattern. For a moment, she met his eyes and smiled.

Her hand flinched.

Brawley was quick, she had to give him that. Even as her hand moved he was throwing his arms up to ward off a conjuring. That was when she darted forward, her clenched fist opening and throwing a handful of salt in his eyes. He barely had time to scream before she'd seized his shirt and slammed her wooden leg between his knees. She rode him to the ground as he folded up, the flailing knife cutting a line of pain in her arm. Knotting her hands in his hair, she cracked his head twice against the stone.

The spinning lanterns dropped as he went limp, rolling on the wet grass and shattering where they hit the slabs. Anna rose, dusting the salt from her hands, and as she did Margaret clawed the fabric from her lips, threw it off her shoulders and ran over to Cora, hugging her tight. They held each other under the tree, rocking back and forth, as the fireflies sparked in the night. "I got you," Margaret whispered. "I got you."

Cora said snaked her arms closer around Margaret and buried her face in her neck. "I thought for sure you'd give him— that you'd have to—"

"How could I?" Margaret said, high color in her cheeks. She gave Cora a quick, hard kiss. "I've already given my heart."

Cora's eyes opened wide in alarm. "Maggie, she's right there."

"It's fine. She says she's been married." Margaret kissed Cora again, slower this time, drawing the other woman close against her. And though she had been married, Anna turned and stared out across the clearing. Her cheeks burned. Nothing to do with me, she told herself. Surely not sisters, and not friends, either. What a world.

At her feet Brawley Gabal's eyelids fluttered, speckled black and burned where the salt had touched him. She kicked the knife out of his hand, just to be certain. He groaned and looked up at her, his face slack. Bloody foam bubbled at the corners of his lips.

"I don't," he gurgled, the words slurred. "Don't… understand. Could have been… happy. Would've been...so happy."

"No," Anna said. "You wouldn't have."

Cranberry vines crunched beside her and Margaret appeared, wrapping the tatters of her shawl around her shoulders, Cora a step or two behind. "You didn't let me finish," she said. She enunciated the words clearly, her brown eyes flashing. "I renounce you, you bastard."

A shiver ran through the leaves and ruffled the petals of the scattered flowers. Brawley twitched on the ground, his fingers curling weakly against the rock. Behind the concussed eyes, a light of naked terror burned. "Friend…'ll find you. He'll… find you."

Anna shook her head. "He's not your friend. Dawn's coming, Brawley Gabal. And I'm sorry, but you promised him a heart."

They left him there, walking across the cracked rocks toward the forest, under black smear of the cloudy sky. The lanterns winked out one by one behind them as they left the clearing, the darkness rolling over the great elm and its twisted roots, scurrying over the bracken. The two women walked close together, trembling with released tension, their hands clamped together like they'd never let go.

Following a step or two behind, Anna thought about the shattered door of their cabin and the wreckage inside, the gleam of Brawley's knife and the terror on Margaret's face beneath the dark trees. An ache squeezed her chest. Now that it was done, she saw all the ways it might have gone wrong, flashing teeth and knives, and her hands trembled. They would look at her and ask the questions they'd been polite enough not to ask, and she would have to answer them. She had no place in that house, she saw now. Better to collect her rucksack and go, leave these strangers to their relief and happiness, fade away—

"Anna," Margaret said, loud, and Anna realized that the small woman was looking at her in the dark, her smile tired and kind. "Will you stay with us a while? We'll make you a bed down beside ours, and feed you hot food. Please. It's the least we can do."

"Oh," Anna said. Her mouth worked for a long moment. Then, shyly, she smiled back. "Of course."

The first spatters of the predawn rains came rolling down as they reached the brushline, with the promise of more to come. Ferns whispered in the breeze, the dark smear of the clouds pressing low overhead. Out behind them a groan rose, weak and faint, and answered by a distant sound, wet and snuffling and eager across the rocks.

"What's that?" Cora said. She made to load the rifle, but Margaret caught her arm and shook her head.

"No concern of ours," Anna said. "Come on. Let's go and get dry."

GHOST DAYS

1903-1904

They walked a while, her and the black dog, long enough that Anna sometimes forgot it was there. It came during hard times, when the road stretched out ahead of her, endless and empty, and she went forward with nothing to look forward to; days when she leaned on her walking stick, hurting in places she hadn't known she could ache, the bag heavy and digging into her shoulders. At times like that, she kept an eye out for it in the waver of the noonday heat, or in the purple texture of the dusk. The shadow in hound shape, pacing her always, eyes glowing in the gloom.

She'd look up from picking roots and leaves for poultices and see it sprawled out in the shadow beneath a tree, utterly still, melting into the shade. Sometimes it was vague shape out in the forest, familiar by the ache in her head, dull and cold as icy metal. Other nights it approached her through the far away trunks, flickering across the intervening space, until it padded beside her, a huge loping thing, shoulders rolling in its great black back, heavy jaws sweeping the ground. A shadow in hound shape, melting in and out of the dark. And then it would go, and she would not see it again. Until the next time.

"He look like a dog, aye," one older man told her, juggling a corncob pipe in his teeth. "Sort of like a dog. But he's not. My granny saw him once on the road back in Somersett, walking her home. Or maybe he was about his own business. Old Shuck is like that. He come and go as he please, and he'll do with you what he like."

"I don't want him," Anna said.

"He wants you," the old man said. "You won't shake him unless he cares to be shook. Better get used to him."

***

Onward, through hill and holler, and everywhere she stopped there was work to be done. Lost things to find and witcheries to dispel, prescriptions of iron horseshoes and doors turned three-times around, and little glass bottles shoved up in chimneys with urine and locks of hair. There were hags to break and spirits to bind, and horrors that crept out through the deep woods or down the high mountains, killed and crept back, with nobody the wiser until they found the bones. And always, there were ghosts.

There was a town where a hanged man's shadow turned on the jailhouse wall, turned and turned in the corner of the eye, though they'd painted the wall over ten times, and might paint it ten times more. Something invisible howled there on the rooftops at morning, on the hanging hour. Something peered and pressed from the other side of the mirror. She unwound it with time; an innocent man sent to the gallows for his lover's death, and the wealthy man responsible drinking himself to a slow demise. Not slow enough. She hauled him out onto the main street of that mirrorless town, as the hanged shadow drifted across the walls toward him, and a crowd screamed at her in fear and rage, and shrank from the mirror in her hand…

There was a sun-drenched glen of azalea and laurel, carpets of fern and moss surrounding a deep pool beneath a waterfall. She stripped and washed her clothing, settling in the shallows and enjoying the warmth of the day on her back, the flutter of butterflies as they lapped salt from her coat. Until a ghost appeared in the water, a naked woman pale as bone, with bruises on her neck. Foam like a white dress on her body, covering it, exposing it, covering it again. Cold lips moving. The current snatched her words away. The light moved and the reflections splintered, like she'd never been there at all. The nuthatches in the trees calling down *poor girl, poor girl, oh the wind and the rain…*

A deep defile beneath the high mountains, where only the midday sun shone. Mist rolling over twisted boulders and twining trees. In that narrow ravine Anna found a desrick with a withered corpse inside, dressed in fine clothes, mummified hands clutched tight around a faded pearlescent stone, the flesh melted into its surface. She did not touch it. Walking back outside of the ruined house she heard a heavy rustling up in the folds of the rock ledges, great scales rasping against each other, and then the lazy hiss of a rattle, like wind in the trees tops, buzzing along her wooden leg, buzzing along her bones…

It all blurred together. A phantom horse exploding from a fireplace, racing around the cabin in a shower of sparks; an iron horseshoe over the fireplace for that. The Bride Deer of Cocke County, blue-eyed, gossamer coated; don't try and shoot it, by god, the bullets will just come back. Diamond Eyes who haunted the still, standing tall and black in the weeping laylock, eyes glinting like a cat: stop drinking or get used to him.

Thick fog on the banks of the French Broad in the mornings, drifting along the floating logs. Trees vanishing beneath the axe and steam saw, forests bleeding out the cuts where the roads go. Red sunsets on steep hillsides. Step by step she went toward the Qualla Boundary, with a vague thought of stopping a time with the Eastern Band of the Cherokee. She did stay there a while, in a home beneath the hills, near where the creek flowed over the pebbles. An old medicine man listening, looking at her and shaking his head.

"You were taught what you were taught," he said. "I hope it's of some use to you. But unless you are going to stay with us, do things the right way—there's things it's not proper you should know. You want recipes, formulas. You want to beat the devil down. Will you stop and learn the old knowledge? All of it? Will you stay here the years it takes to learn? We don't do what you want to know how to do, sister. I think you best go your own way."

There'd been words said it was hard to take back. She left Cherokee town and set out again on her own, angry, so angry, swallowed up by the thing that urged her on, drove her to stand eye to eye with every horror she could find. And at night—on floors, in brush, in lean-tos—she dreamed of past faces, and horrors that made her crash awake, cold and still and aching. But not dead. Not yet.

***

Anna and the black dog walked. Sometimes it led, ranging out in front of her until it dwindled at the end of the path. Sometimes following, and never far behind. She thought sometimes about a cold bald under the moon, the rumble and break of timber, a whisper of souls escaping into the breeze. *You owe me.* Wondered if she'd laid a debt on something by accident, a debt now being paid in some way she couldn't fathom. Or perhaps there was something in her that drew it out: the cold metal feeling in her head, the mornings when rising was almost more than she could bear.

One day she didn't get up at all. She was lying in a mountain field in springtime, inside a bowl-shaped valley surrounded on all sides by the ridgelines. The world was too heavy, pressing down like a boot on her back, and the road was too long. A day and night she lay in the grass, like she might never move again. And then the Black Shuck was beside her, stretched out like it had always been there: shaggy and black and vague, as if she could blink it away. A waiting, intent feeling, like it was watching to see what she would do.

"Go away," she said into the dirt.

The great head cocked over her. Long jaws opened. Then teeth squeezed gently around her neck, the skin of her collarbone prickling under strands of shaggy hair. Prickled and burned, cold as ice.

She dug her hands into the dirt and pushed herself up, slow. The jaws retreated as she did, teeth keeping their soft touch on her skin, until the great head nestled against her breast, twisted up against her. She was so cold that her teeth chattered.

"No," she said. "Not… yet."

And then she was alone there in the field, the sun hanging low in the sky. The ground was littered with paw-prints larger than her hand, circling in excitement, or frustration, or some alien emotion she could not fathom.

She pushed herself up and went on. Walking still, down the ghost days. Never walking away.

SPEAKING WITH TSUL'KALU

1904

The morning after they laid her husband down, Anna O'Brien woke to find him sitting by her bed. She surfaced slowly, the sleep sliding off her, and all was normal: the sunlight pooling on the linens and painting the wall-quilt, drawing a creamy glow from the year-old cabin timbers, and Tom O'Brien, smiling, his lanky body draped over the rough chair. Joy crashed over her and for a moment she floated in the warmth, staring at his smile. The physical pain that followed was nothing—not the scratches, not the aches in her muscles, not even the throbbing tingle of her missing left leg. She looked at Tom, drawing the sight of his plain, pleasant face around her like a blanket. The horror and rage of the past night, the glint of firelight on bone, long white limbs stalking through the black trees—all of it drained away. If he was there, it had worked. As long as he was there, it could not touch her.

But it did. It came over her slowly, as her neighbors bustled in, gave her water to sip and laid food on the table. They spoke to her in hesitant voices and she barely spoke back, busy drinking in the sight of Tom sitting there on the chair, watching over her, solid Tom, his broad-brimmed hat and coat hooked to one side. The room pulsed, a slow dance of light and shadow from the swaying branches outside, keeping time to the throb of her heartbeat. And gradually it came to Anna that the shadow of his hat and coat lay blue and alone on the floor; that Tom didn't speak back; that something was terribly wrong there in the sunlit cabin.

She didn't need them to tell her he was dead. She knew.

***

Darkness. Emptiness spun around her, pressing in at all sides. She drifted there, letting it, the sensations crawling over her motionless body. The hat held lightly between her fingers. The slow, soundless flap of the battered coat against her sides, tangled hair brushing her face. Nothing to do but hang there. Nothing to do but remember; sunlight dripping along the carvings in the rock, the burr of the cicadas, her dry tongue filling her mouth on the fourth day of the fast. Or had it been the sixth? Or had it been the moment when the carvings began to dance before her weary eyes, the pictographs spinning and shifting in alien patterns, circling the great seven-fingered handprint?

Perhaps she'd died. She'd reached for the swirling carvings, tumbling forward and down, through the green grass and into the dark. What had she been trying to do? A week spent before an old slab of grey stone in a mountain cove, without food, water, or sleep. Something about a door. Something about ice over deep water. Something about–

"Judaculla," she said.

A ripple ran through the black. Something whispered against her face, cool and unfamiliar, and she squinted at it, trying to work out what it was. Only as her clothing shifted and pulled against her body did she realize that it was moving air, and that she was falling.

She collided with solid ground a second later, her boots slipping out from under her, reeling her backward in an instant of blind disorienting panic before her hip and elbow cracked against wet stone. She rolled onto her side, curling away from the pain, breath hissing from between clenched teeth. The hunger and thirst were gone, left behind in the world above. In their place was a sharp, urgent agony in her joints.

She clung to the feeling, forced herself to think, to take stock. The darkness around her was impenetrable, but she thought she sensed a gravity to it now, a nearly imperceptible tug of confined air. The faint echo of dripping water touched her ears. A cave, perhaps. A slick-floored cave, as her elbows were keenly reminding her. The worst pressed in close behind; deep crevasses of jagged rock, bottomless lakes, the guts of a mountain holding her til nothing remained but bones in the endless black.

She hissed out another breath and pushed the thought away, hauling herself to her knees. Light, that was the first thing; something to help her get her bearings. With one hand, she pulled a pair of fire stones from one worn pocket of the coat, retrieving a small plug of tinder from the other. Setting the tinder against the tip of her boot, she rested her hands atop her foot and struck the fire stones together. Sparks flared up, nesting in the tinder. She struck again, and this time it caught, little tongues of yellow fire spreading over the tangle of tree bark and oakum. Light raced along the floor, washing up spiraling columns and vast shelves of glistening stone, washing up—

"*Put that out.*"

The darkness fell back in on her, impossibly huge. She didn't even have time to cry out in shock; the next instant she was slammed back against the rock and pinned by something huge and leathery. The terrible voice sizzled on the air, deep enough to rattle Anna's bones. "Seven days and nights you spent fasting at my rock. I open the door, and you have the gall to make *light*. Who are you?"

"Conjure-woman," Anna wheezed. "Anna O'Brien. Are you Judaculla?"

"That is two insults you have offered great Tsul'kalu," snarled the voice. The weight on top of Anna ground down, merciless, crushing the air from her lungs. Her ribs creaked sickeningly inside her chest. She opened her mouth, trying to speak, but no sound came out. Her foot jerked and the pressure eased, just enough for her to suck in a breath. The smell that came with it was strong enough to taste, an overwhelming stew of musk and lightning and fresh-killed meat. "Two. There will not be a third. Did you come to stare, I wonder? A pale little thing like you must be *curious*."

Anna's head spun. "Ary offense I gave, I'm sorry. But I'm not… so pale. I've got the Cherokee blood, from my mother and grandfather both. From way back."

"Blood?" Laughter rumbled like thunder in the black. The leather flesh pressed against Anna's face, pregnant with threat. "Your blood does not make you *Aniyunwiya*. The true tribe knew the rituals and the words. Only the holiest came to speak to me, carried on rivers of prayer into the land-beneath-mountains, and only the bravest hunters earned my favor in the chase. They knew to come in darkness and respect! What do *you* know?"

Her shaking hands balled into fists. "I've settled haints and hags—"

"Nothing, then. Better to have walked into the forest and died, little conjure-woman. You'd have found your best use in the bellies of bird and beast. Better there than alone, beneath the hand of Tsul'kalu."

"Then do it."

Leathery skin rasped against her face. "Do it?"

"Do it!" The words flew from Anna's mouth before she had a chance to stop them, sharp and flat as obsidian. "Go on! You want rituals? You want words? I came up in a holler fifty years after they marched the tribe out! Nobody told me the *words!* Everything I've done, I've done on my own, and by god, I won't be toyed with. Not by some spirit I don't hardly know. Go on now, goddamn you! *Judaculla!*"

Her heart thundered in her throat, waiting for the palm to slam forward, to smash and break her against the rock. But the great hand atop her never moved. It seemed to hang there an age, as she sucked in breath after breath, knowing each would be her last. Then, suddenly, it was gone.

She lay there a moment longer before pulling herself into a sitting position. Fumbling at her trouser leg, she wrenched it up and ran her hand along the wooden shin of her left leg, feeling for cracks. A strange mixture of anger and embarrassment at her outburst prickled inside her. "I'm sorry," she muttered. "I'm sorry. That's not your name."

"Anna O'Brien." The ozone crackle faded away, leaving behind a voice like that of a man. "You are a fool. A brave fool, but a fool. You fasted at the stone of a strange spirit, without the proper prayers or reflection to guide you. The spirit world is cruel to those who do not know its ways. You would have been lost to the void had I not plucked you out. And I . . . do not like the light."

"Sure," Anna said. "That's sure a reason to near kill someone."

"The anger of Tsul'Kalu is a fearful thing," rumbled the voice. "Like storms, rolling across the slopes. But storms pass. Tell me: why did you come here to die?"

"I didn't."

"Didn't you?" said the spirit. "I know the look of welcomed death. The exhaustion of the flight, when you have run too long and can run no more, and what follows is close behind. The buck falls to the wolves, the rabbit to the hawk. And you? I see it in your gaze."

The rock under Anna twisted, softened, flowed up around her fingers. She flinched and climbed unsteadily to her feet, dirt tumbling from her shaking hands. High above, the darkness faded into a velvet starscape, the ink draining out of the air to be replaced by a rich palette of blues and greys. Only one shadow remained; a giant seated figure, with vast slanting shoulders and shaggy flanks, outlined like mountain crags against the dusk. The great head shifted, moonlight glinting off of huge eyes.

"You have fought spirits, little conjure-woman," said Tsul'kalu. "You have banished them. I wonder if you have ever tried speaking with them."

***

Anna did not talk with spirits. In her first months on the road, she hardly spoke with anyone, and had to force herself to start. It was that or fail in what she'd set for herself, fail in learning what she needed to know. She threw herself into the work; herbs to pick and poultices to make, hermits and cunning-folk to seek out, woodcraft and witchcraft to practice. In time she found in herself an unexpected knack for talking, for prying without seeming to pry, for remembering gossip and telling stories, and she practiced whenever she could. But never with haints or hags, and never with spirits. She might bind them, and she might threaten them; that was all. To do otherwise would grant them something she was unwilling to give.

But spectral things often spoke to her. She was in an old barn in the high hills of Santeetlah, settling a spirit. It fluttered around her as she worked, a man-shaped quiver in the musty air, stirring the pollen on the stacks of lumber and tools. It whispered a promise in her ear about a stone in a cove valley far to the east, polished by wind and by long-dead hands, where the great spirits moved into the mortal world, and mortals could sometimes move back.

"Not interested," she told it, drawing the last line on the floor.

"Cruel," sighed the voice. Pollen and dust danced through sunlit shafts. "Even to me, giving advice. Even, I hear to your poor husband—"

She thrust her hand forward and exhaled, and a moment later the ghost was gone, the voice fading, the air empty and still. When she left the rotting barn and took her money from the farmhand, she struck out through the backwoods away from the road, forcing her way up the steep slopes until her heart throbbed and her breath rang harsh in her throat.

That night, lying beneath a tangled brush fall, Anna dreamed an old dream; of a lost sea, cold and still beneath the rock, blackness above the water, blackness below. She cast off her clothes and sank, her wooden leg dragging her down, down into the dark. When she woke, damp with sweat beside the rotting logs, she thought again about the ghost's words. Without quite knowing why, she crawled out, hauled her pack on her shoulder and headed east through the gloom, toward the rising sun.

In between odd jobs, she began to ask after the stone. At first, nobody seemed to know what she was talking about. She kept on, asking everybody she met, as the slopes rose and fell, and the green Balsam Mountains spread over the distance. She shrugged when people asked why she was looking for it. Curiosity, she told them, and privately, she thought it must be something like that. But there was something deeper, too. A tight lump in her belly and a restless hunger in her heart, a gnawing sensation drawing her down the winding road.

She found what she was looking for outside of Cullowhee. It was a hot day, the sun beating down from a cloudless sky, and by a crooked footbridge Anna came upon a young woman washing clothing in the creek. The girl smiled as soon as she approached, delighted for company. Soon

Anna was sitting on the bank beside her, good foot dangling in the cool water, helping with the scrubbing.

"I dunno for sure," the girl said, rolling her thick shoulders before returning to the washboard. Her name was Vandy, and she had nut brown hair and a constellation of freckles over her broad face. Yellow curls of pollen whirled away from the shirt she dunked in the creek. "But I think you want the Judaculla Rock. It ain't far from here. I heard all about it from my Paw Paw."

"What'd he tell you?"

Vandy laughed. "Oh, lots. He said it was a rock so old that even the Cherokee don't know who carved it, and that whoever did left it as a stepping stone for wild gods. Signed and sealed it with a seven-fingered hand. Now Judaculla, he had seven fingers, so I guess that's why it's his? He was some old devil from before the white man came. You get lots of that around the mountains, I think. Old stories."

Anna's mouth quirked. "You do at that," she said. "It's close?"

"Sure. Everyone around here knows it. People passing it at night say they hear knocking, or folks talking from far away." Vandy tossed the last of her laundry into the basket. "You get travelling folk who fall asleep next to it, sometimes, but they never stay long. Sleeping under that rock's like running your hand on ice over deep water. You can feel it creaking, and who knows what's down there?"

"I hear you can go inside and find out," Anna said.

"You got to fast and pray a whole week to open that door, Paw-Paw said. A whole week! But I guess if it was easy, anybody'd do it. You got the Cherokee blood, you said? I reckon you should go look. Walk a few miles down Old Cullowhee Road, and left on Caney Fork Road, over the creek bottoms. You'll find it easy enough."

The trees closed in around her as she went down into the cove valley, basswood and redbuds swaying in the late afternoon haze. The rock itself stood in a gently sloping clearing; a great slab of soapstone, worn by time and the elements, matted grasses and clovers tangled at its base. Its surface shone with a faintly oily sheen in the sunset light, dapples of blue shadow spilling along faint carvings in the rock. The longer Anna looked at them, the less sense they made to her—a spidery network of curling lines and circles, fading in and out of focus. Shapes unlike anything she'd ever seen in the waking world. Finally, she shook her head and looked away.

"Alright," she said. "I'm here. What now?"

Crickets thrummed in the fields. The rock stood, sloping and silent in the dim light. Anna took a last drink from her water bottle, and drained the rest out onto the grass. Then she sat before the stepping stone of the spirits, closed her eyes, and prepared to step back.

***

Tin, lukewarm water. Sweet pollen clogging her nose. For a moment she wasn't sure where she was, or when she was; then the sensations were gone, snatched away as if by a sudden wind, and she stood again in long grass. The world around her was picked out in sharp lines and washes of moonlight, revealing spiraling trunks that wound toward the sky, upside-down ferns hanging in tangled canopies from leafless branches.

"What was that?" she said, wobbling a moment.

"*Usunhi'yi*," the spirit rumbled. No light shone where Tsul'kalu sat, granite-shouldered and still, face hidden in shadow, save its eyes, which glowed faintly in the black. "Here in the land-beneath-mountains, there are pathways that lead through the mind, to be traveled with a thought. And you, little conjure-woman, think loud thoughts."

Anna paced through the spirit grass, the bent stalks unfolding and straightening behind her feet. "We were in a cave—"

"I brought us up beneath a sky," Tsul'kalu said. "I thought you might find it more to your liking. Now. Why do you want to die?"

The grass mumbled against her legs. "I really don't."

"You were ready to die in the cave."

"I was hungry and tired and scared," Anna said. "And I was tired of playing games with you."

In the distance, the glowing eyes narrowed. "People speak to the spirits because they want things. You took on the fast and vigil to come here, and might have died doing so. You say you do not want this. What is so important to you that you would risk a death you do not want?"

"I guess… this." Anna lowered herself carefully onto her knees. She thought for a moment, trying to put it into words. "I had to see all this for myself. I was raised God-fearing, but you know, I never see any of him. Just devils and old ghosts. That's all I seen for . . . well. I figured they had to come and go from somewhere. Somewhere real."

She had the sudden sense that the giant was weighing her from his seat on the horizon. She shifted uncomfortably, caught herself, and sat stock still. "Great Tsul'kalu," she said. "I come seeking knowledge."

"Knowledge," said the spirit, drawing the word out. The syllables cracked together like tumbling stones. "You go to Kana'ti or Red Man-Woman for knowledge, little conjure-woman. I am Tsul'Kalu, the Lord of Game. My thoughts are simple thoughts. Trade me for them."

"What?"

"Show me what you believed. You spoke of God," the spirit said. "I do not know him. Show him to me now."

"I can't show you anything!" Anna felt a strange note of panic; she had neither cracked a bible nor entered a church for nearly three years, and remembered only a handful of verses she'd used on a particularly stubborn ghost. "That's the point."

"*Usunhi'yi*." A note of growling impatience sounded in Tsul'kalu's voice. "You are in the spirit world, and you think… loud thoughts. Think of this, and show me."

Anna took a deep breath. "Alright," she said. "In the beginning—"

***

In the beginning, there was the camp. Some towns had churches; some towns had preachers, paid ones, who stayed and gave sermons every Sabbath. For everyone else living scattered in the hills, religion came in the camp communion, held when the harvest was in, or when a charismatic blew through on a revival wind. They packed up enough clothes and food for a few days and came down, sometimes traveling for miles, until they all converged on some dusty field, where arbors rose old and cracked beneath the sun. Anyone could stand there beneath the shade and testify to the greatness of God; anyone could hear the hum of the Word from a hundred lips, and know that no one in the world was more blessed than they.

The Kinnonas lived in a saddleback notch with three other families, and seldom saw their neighbors. Anna's father came home rarely, and when he did his cough was a hacking eruption in the little cabin, his arms twisted and aching from his work in the mines and the mills. Her mother was worn down, with heavy eyes and a quick temper; the younger children ran wild in their father's absence. Anna kept to herself. She had always been quiet; quiet and serious, doing what needed doing, and keeping out of the way.

But there were always the camp days, when the Kinnonas loaded up their grandfather's wagon with tents and blankets and bounced down the pitted track in a line with the other three households, until they came to the field where everyone had gathered. There the whole camp prayed and sang, and when the praying and singing were done, they cooked and gossiped. Then they lit fires in the dust and danced to keening fiddle and banjo, man and wife, old and young, the unwed boys passing and catching the breathless girls.

And somewhere Tom O'Brien caught her, tall and handsome, with his open face and beard that never quite came in. Two camp meetings they danced, Tom passing her away and returning, plucking her up in his strong arms and whirling her down the line to the high skirling strings, her dress soaked with sweat, his high laugh ringing out until she couldn't help but laugh with him. Two camp meetings they walked off in the dark, talking. On the third his hard fingers wrapped around hers and he kissed her the first time against the side of her family's wagon, his shine-breath tingling against her lips. And Anna Kinnona, fifteen years old, solemn and watchful, who'd seen her parents talking in low voices when they thought the children were asleep, who'd noted the scarcity of food on the bent tin plates at suppertime and the worn, hopeless look on her father's face—Anna twined her fingers in his hair and kissed him back.

The next year they were married at the camp. A hot breeze kicked up the dust on the day, driving white curtains across the dry grass. Anna and Tom gathered, surrounded by other families, the fifth couple that day to get married and by no means the last. She hugged her parents, grinning, and kissed Tom to widespread cheers. And then at camp's end, Tom took her away on a borrowed cart loaded with wedding gifts, the wedding quilt rolled up between them, leaving her parents and siblings behind. Riding there beside him she felt free and terrified and grateful to be gone.

He'd built them a cabin on a hillside in the steep woodlands beneath cliffs of sandstone granite, twenty-five miles, thirteen creeks and a world away from her parents home. "I started building it the first time I danced with you," he said, as the cart clattered up the the last leg of the track.

Anna cocked her head at him. "How did you know I'd say yes?"

"I just knew," he said. "I saw you and I just knew you had to be my wife. If I couldn't have you, I think I'd have died. And I sure wasn't gonna marry you if I didn't have someplace to for the two of us."

"I might have said no," she said. "Pa might've said no."

"You're here," he said. "So I guess I was right."

But though she smiled and kissed his cheek, she felt a flicker of disquiet. It was like he was still swirling her through the line, content that he knew the steps. But how could he know? How could anyone really know? The fiddler called the tune and you danced, for two years the same dance. But what happened when the dance changed? What happened if the day came when she didn't like the steps anymore?

He drew up the cart by the house, swept her up in his arms and kissed her cheek. "Come on, Anna O'Brien," he said. And then he carried her over the threshold, her feet never touching the ground, carried her straight over the pale boards and straight over to the bed. "We can go way down to county courthouse in the morning. But morning's pretty far away."

***

The taste of him left her lips, evaporating away with the dust of the camp and singsong cry of the preacher's voice. Anna shivered, there in the night-draped forest, and hugged her arms together. The grass twined and curled about her thighs. "That didn't answer your question, I guess."

"Didn't it?" said Tsul'Kalu. "God-fearing is a world without spirits. And you came here because you are not god-fearing anymore."

Anna's mouth tightened. "The trade's done. Now tell me about—" she fumbled over the word for a moment. "*Usunhi'yi*. The spirit world. What's its shape? What lives here?"

An immense arm lifted on the horizon, pointing long fingers. "Everything. We sit in the counter-country, through which all things must pass, and where all things find their end. Now. Were you god-fearing with your husband?"

"I don't want to talk about my husband," Anna said.

"Why not?"

"Because you've never been married," she said. "You ever been in love? You understand it? Frankly, I don't feel inclined toward making you try. My husband's my business, not yours. Don't ask about him again."

The tree trunks shifted in the shadows, and for a moment the grass wound tighter against her legs. Above her the spirit loomed, still and heavy as a mountain, and Anna again had the sense of being measured, her soul field-dressed and laid out before the spirit's gaze. Her flesh crawled, and for a moment she wondered if she'd gone too far.

Finally, Tsul'kalu spoke. "You have told me two tales. Now I will tell you one, from long ago. And you can decide what I know and what I don't."

***

Know this; it happened in the old days, when the Principle People were fresh down from the north, coming by waves down the great valleys and burrowing up into the hills. They settled in towns on the river-bottoms, tilling their crops and hunting in the woodlands. Those were the legend times, when the medicine people went into the deep woods and up onto the high peaks, to smoke pipes with the land's spirits and gain their favor. For the mounds of Kotani had fallen and its nations had scattered; there were great powers in the woods, and not all of them meant the People well.

In a glade at Känuga Town, there lived a beautiful young woman named Ahyoka and her widowed mother. Though Ahyoka wanted desperately to be married, her mother rejected her suitors, telling her that she must only take a good hunter for a husband, someone who could keep them fed through the long winters. Ten men had come courting, and ten men her mother had turned away. After the last left, Ahyoka went to go sleep in the little winter house across from the cabin, wishing under her breath for a hunter that nobody, not even her mother could refuse.

The trees rustled. The night winds gusted, ruffling the waters until they sang their secret song. And the next night, as Ahyoka sat fuming outside the winter house, a man came walking out of the dark.

"I've heard of you," said the man. He was tall and well shaped, with long ropes of muscle and strong fingers. On his back he held a great buck, its neck broken and limp. "I've heard you're lovely as the sun running across the sky. I'm lonely in my own country. I'll marry you, if you'll have me."

"I might," Ahyoka said. "But my mother says she'll only let me marry a great hunter."

The man's teeth glinted white. "A great hunter? I am the best." He dropped the deer on the ground. "May I come in?"

Ahyoka looked him over again, and smiled. "You may," she said, and pulled him inside the winter house. She felt an urgent desire come over her, ravenous and hungry, and she collapsed back into the sheets of her cabin bed—but there was no cabin. Just the winter house, and the man, and the dark.

He left before morning's first light faded over the trees, telling her he had to return to his own country. When her mother awoke she exclaimed over the deer, astounded at its size and the lack of arrow wounds. Together they skinned and dressed it, dining well on the meat and storing the rest. And when night had fallen and Ahyoka's mother had gone to bed, the man came back. This time he had a deer over each shoulder, which he dropped on the ground as he came with her into the winter house.

Night after night, he came to her bed; night after night he slipped away before sunrise, before Ahyoka or her mother could study him in the light of day. He brought them meat, deer and elk and bear. When her mother asked for wood, they woke to find great trees torn up by the roots and splintered into pieces, stacked neatly beside the two houses. The people of Känuga dined well on the meat the hunter brought, for the family soon had more than they knew what to do with. Ahyoka was happy, and ignored their questions about her mysterious husband. But her mother fretted.

"He never waits," she finally said. "He never stays. I've never even seen him. What kind of son-in-law do I have?"

"A good hunter," Ahyoka said.

Her mother did not look pleased. "Hunting isn't everything. I want to see him."

That night, as the tree frogs croaked and the waters babbled, Ahyoka told her husband what her mother had said. When he heard the words he frowned, his eyes slanting in the firelight. "Why?" he said. "I'll frighten her. I'm not always… handsome in the light. Doesn't she like the deer?"

"She says hunting isn't everything. Look, just stay a little while in the morning. Just a little while. I haven't seen you either, great hunter. I want to see what sort of man I'm marrying, too."

He chewed that over and sighed. "She must not scream. Or call me frightful."

"She won't." Ahyoka hugged him and kissed his jaw. Something twisted inside her, confused, and then was gone. "Come to bed."

The night passed. The sun rose over the treetops. She woke with the sun and heard her mother hammering on the wall outside with the flat of her hand. "Pull your blankets up! I want to see him." Even as Ahyoka rolled over her mother stepped inside, sending the sunlight flooding in. She did not quite see what happened next. She had a brief glimpse of something huge and matted curled up in the winter house, its head jammed against one end of the roof, its toes curled at the other. Behind her, her mother screamed in shock. Quick as thought, the huge thing rose in a blur of movement, tearing through the wall and roof.

"You were warned!" snarled a voice like lightning. Branches and daub rained down on Ahyoka's head. "I go back to my own land. Your mother, your village—they will never see me now." And then he was gone, leaving only the wreckage of the winter house behind him.

Ahyoka did not speak to her mother for three days. On the fourth day her body was wracked by terrible spasms, so painful that she screamed through gritted teeth. All night long she moaned and wept there in the summer house, her mother mopping her forehead with wet moss. In the morning she found her sheets soaked with a huge mass of black and red blood, almost solid to the touch. Her mother gathered the blankets up and washed the blood off in the river, scraping it off in huge curling masses that floated away down the current. "I don't know who your husband was," she said when she returned, "but I think you're well rid of him."

Ahyoka was not so sure. By day she was listless, staring off into the mountains, and there were those in Känuga who said that she was spirit-touched, and could never again be part of the human world. Every night she found herself waiting beside the ruin of the winter house, hoping he would come.

Finally, he did. She was sitting beside the broken wall, and suddenly he was there beside her, wearing a face both strange and achingly familiar. "You are alone, my wife?"

"You left," she said. "Of course I'm alone."

"I found this in the river," her husband said. He lifted his hand and opened it, seven fingers splayed out. Wiggling in the middle was a worm. "I found it in a great mass of blood, knotted up in the roots of a tree." Ahyoka looked at him, confused. But when she looked at his hand once more she saw he held not a worm but a child, a fat baby girl with walnut skin and slanting eyes. Her daughter.

"My mother," she whispered. "She didn't know."

"She did not know." Her husband hissed through his curved teeth. "Come away with me, my sun. Come away to my country beneath the mountains, and away from these people who cannot see me, and who treat our child so."

She left him sitting there and went to say goodbye to her mother. Then they walked away in the dark, her and her daughter and her husband. And with each step her husband grew larger, his legs longer, his hair spreading down his shoulders and over his body, until finally he was carrying her in his hand, the thunder of his passing echoing over the gorges. A great mountain rose ahead, and as they approached a great hole opened in its side, blacker than the inside of the winter hut, blacker than black ink.

Once she was inside, Ahyoka knew, the sun would not touch her again. But was she Ahyoka? The name felt wrong on her, suddenly, ill-fitting. The closer they came to the great door in the mountain, the more something in her strained and kicked to get free. She felt a strange double echo of herself, there in the giant's hand, a woman of Känuga town and a woman from a saddleback holler. She wanted to ask her husband what was happening. But her husband was dead.

And at that thought the second woman inside clawed up inside her, and Anna O'Brien stood and said "No."

***

"No?" said Tsul'Kalu.

They were back in the midnight forest, and Anna tore the memories of another world and another life off of her. She rounded on her wooden heel, hands shaking, her face hot. "No," she hissed. "What do you think you're doing? Making me—making me live that—"

The mountain-shaped thing in the distance leaned down toward her, blotting out the stars. Its great eyes glowed down on her, and when she tried to meet them her eyes seared and she was forced to look away. "Memories are contagious here, conjure woman," the voice boomed, and the ozone crackle ran once again underneath. "A great spirit honors you with his attention, and this is how you repay him? With insults and slights? Mighty Tsul'Kalu taught you a lesson. You seek oblivion? It is here! It can swallow you with a thought! You can be lost so deep you would never climb your way out."

"I remember your *attention!*" Anna gave a little wobbling hop of pure rage, stumbling forward with teeth bared. "Was this your plan? Was this why you plucked me out? Plucking yourself up a new wife?"

"Don't you feel it?" The spirit's whisper was a wind on the branches, and the under-ferns crackled and fell, fronds drifting around

Anna like feathers, bathed in sickly yellow light. "To be in the dark down the long years, alone, carrying them with you? The ones you lost? What do you have out there in the waking world?"

"A life!" Anna snarled.

"A hunted life. Hard and short." The spirit's breath coiled around her face, insinuating and electric. "You carry so many memories, so many dreams. Down here you can live in them. Bathe in them! Never let them go! Don't you love your husband? You can have him. You can have him back."

"*I don't want him back!*"

Silence, there beneath the stars. Anna's hands flew to her mouth. She rocked there for a moment, staring at nothing as the fronds floated around her, her stomach tumbling, tumbling, and never reaching the bottom.

"Ah," breathed Tsul'kalu.

Anna leaned against a nearby tree, her head in her hands. Something ached deep inside her, wriggling and twisting as she tried to dig it out. "I loved him," she said, her voice very small. "I love him. So much. But he's dead. He's dead, and I banished him."

Tsul'kalu sat still as stone, waiting.

"I was lying in bed after my leg came off, and Tom was sitting there alive. But I knew he wasn't, and it was—it was too much. And I just… breathed out. I sent him away." Her voice failed her a moment. She swallowed and kept on, forcing the words through. "And I've tried. God, I've tried to set it right. I've tried to see that the same fate doesn't fall on others, that nobody has to make the trade like I did. But I look back on who I was before, and I don't know her. What kind of person sends their own husband away? What kind of monster?"

The world flickered. The stars dimmed, receding into a wash of paler blue, ripples of strange light playing in ribbons across the vault of the sky. Warm morning sunlight touched Anna's back. Around her the world snapped into focus, bright and clear and sharp. Every stalk, every spinning mote of dust, every shadow under the rustling flowers–she saw them all, the colors burning her eyes. And as she turned to take it all in, she beheld the spirit.

The highest trees of the canopy barely reached its waist. It loomed above her, a wall of tangled red hair dangling from sloping shoulders, long arms planted to either side, squat legs crossed beneath a massive belly. A misshapen face peered down, scarred lips twisting around jutting fangs. And beneath heavy brows, the eyes—slanting, golden eyes, shining with the terrible intensity of a hawk. The eyes of Tsul'Kalu.

How long Anna met that gaze, she could not say. Long enough that her shaking hands stilled and her heartbeat slowed, and warmth rose up inside her, slow and welcome as sunrise. Finally she shook her head, closed her eyes, and drew a deep breath. "Thank you," she said. "I know you don't like the light."

"I do not," said the spirit. "Now. You asked for knowledge. Would you hear the wisdom of the Lord of Game, He Who Has Them Slanting, the most mighty Tsul'Kalu?"

Anna sat up straight. "I would."

"I cannot offer you peace." The huge brow lowered, eyes narrowing. "I cannot offer you certainty. Those are gifts given by cleverer spirits than I. But I can tell you about change. You have changed with his death? You would have changed if he'd lived. It is simple knowledge, hard-won; all things change. Hold on to the past, and you will drown in it. You will throw yourself needlessly toward death; you will kill yourself from shame and misery, and you will help no one, and you will not help him."

"Did she change?" Anna said. "Ahyoka?"

"Of course." Tsul'kalu's lips worked over its fangs. "She lived here, in the land-beneath-mountains, and we had many fine children. But in time they left, and she left too. She wanted to see the true sun again, and so she went. And I… stayed."

The spirit rose slowly, great legs thrusting his body upward, heavy and inevitable as a rising peak. The sky faded away; the grass melted around Anna's feet. Then the twisted trunks began to wink out, one by one, faster and faster, and the darkness grew, swallowing them up, until the light was gone. She found herself again on slick rock, blind, with no sound but the distant echo of dripping water.

"No more," whispered the voice. "No more. It is time for you to go, I think."

"One more thing." She sat there, trying to decide how best to shape the words, how to ask. Finally, she swallowed and spoke. "You said everything comes to *Usunhi'yi* in the end. Everything that ever was. Does that include the dead?"

She could not see the spirit's eyes in the dark, but she felt them on her just the same.

"Yes," Tsul'Kalu said. For the briefest of moments, his voice was gentle. "But you will never find him. Not if you walk for an age through the darkness to the west."

"I . . ." Anna said. She exhaled slowly and closed her eyes. "He's gone. He's been gone. I just needed to know."

"Then I leave you with this," said the spirit. " I am not what I was before man came. I am not what I was before her, and I am not what I will be when all of you are gone. But I am Tsul'Kalu. I am always Tsul'Kalu." There was the scrape of claws in the dark. A series of shining lines etched across the blackness, following the outline of a massive seven-fingered hand. "Walk on, Anna O'Brien. And remember."

The glowing shape filled her vision. She reached toward it, her fingers spread, and felt a prickle as the rippling light spread over her body. She stepped forward and fell, through an eternity of white and the snapping of a second, a last taste of bone and lightning fading from her lungs. A moment later she landed in heat and dry grass, and crumpled in the long blue shadow of the Judaculla Rock, broken open and reborn beneath the vault of the wide blue sky.

Weariness crashed over her like a wave, overwhelming hunger and thirst rushing close behind. She hauled herself up on aching muscles, her legs shaking violently under her weight, and hobbled over to her bag in the long grass, fumbling for the water bottle. She groaned as she realized it was empty.

"Lordy," said a bright voice. Vandy appeared from around the rock, the resurrection ferns crunching under her bare feet. "You look a sight. Don't you look a sight! Here. Have some water."

The rim of a canteen pressed against her cracked lips. For a moment she gulped greedily, water streaming from either side of her mouth, the cold liquid blasting across her tongue like the taste of heaven. Then she got control of herself and took long, level sips until she shook her head and took a breath.

"I wondered how you were doing," Vandy said. "I came by a few days after we met and saw you sitting beneath the rock, so I figured I'd let you alone. But me and Paw Paw, we wondered how you're getting on. I guessed it was a week, and came to see. You must be real hungry! You want to come stay with us a spell? Have some supper? You look like you could use some supper."

"I could at that," Anna said. She pulled herself up and leaned against the girl's shoulder. A wave of dizziness rolled over her and she staggered, caught herself, and laughed. Something inside her had broken open, a weight she'd hardly noticed before, or perhaps a weight she'd told herself that she did not have. A tangled lump of regret and doubt and terror. I am not what I was, she thought. How about that.

"Hang on now," Vandy said. "So you ever get down there under the rock? What'd you see, anyway?"

"Enough," Anna said. "I think… I think I saw enough."

***

Months after they laid her husband down, Anna dressed herself in his clothes. She had paced the walls of the cabin a thousand times now; first with her neighbors holding her arms, getting her used to walking on her new wooden leg, and then by herself, back and forth over the wooden boards, night and day, until she hardly wobbled. Yet the walls had closed in around her as the days passed—Tom's cabin, built with his own hands. There were times sitting at the table when she could hardly breathe, when the bed spat her out and she had to go sleep in a bundle of blankets on the cold porch.

Someone would take her back if she asked. The neighbors had surely been talking about it, the young widow alone up in that empty cabin. Someone would offer to hitch a wagon and take her back up the pitted roads, across the creeks and through the winding passes. She could go back to the saddleback notch, and everything could be like it was, minus two years and one leg. Everything could be normal again.

She just had to ask.

Instead she piled his clothes out on the floor. She had spent the first months of her convalescence sewing and cutting, trimming some of them down until they fit her. Wearing them only when alone, shaking her head when Milly O'Brien asked her what she was doing. Now she pulled on a pair of trousers and a work shirt, slipping his boots on over her feet, slicing into the left one until she could get her wooden leg inside. Finally, she went over to the coat and hat hanging on the chair and pulled them on, the fabric and felt settling on her like a weight.

On went the laden rucksack she'd left on the table, swinging on her shoulder. Into her hand went the walking stick she'd whittled herself while in bed. She crossed to the door and opened it, the cool air flooding in, heavy with the smell of lilac and pine and the bur of night insects. She paused there a moment and looked back into the dark cabin, staring at the room, the empty bed with its tangle of sheets, the smoldering coals of the fireplace. Not too late to go back, she knew. Not yet.

For a moment, Anna O'Brien's hand lingered on the latch.

But the thought passed. She tilted the hat down over her eyes and shrugged the pack higher up on her back. Then she was gone, the door shut firmly behind her. Gone, into the dark.

AFTERWORD

Some characters come to you from inspiration. Anna O'Brien came about as part of a decision. It was 2010, and I was in my senior year of high school. I'd already managed to write and publish a few short stories, most of them ending up in low-paying (but wonderfully accepting) outlets like Bards and Sages. I had a vague idea that I wanted to write about an Appalachian mountain man, the sort of wandering character who could hold down a series. But no matter how I tried, it just wasn't coming. The whole thing felt rote, uninteresting. He'd have a beard, I guessed? A rifle? Please.

Then I had a thought: what if the character were a woman? She would be… a grifter, a conjure-woman, and she would have one leg, the other lost to some strange mountain sorcery. She would wear a big hat that hid her eyes, more often than not, and a big coat. The more I thought about the idea, the more I liked it; I immediately scrapped whatever story I was working on and started plotting a story about the character. (That story never got off the ground because it turned into a novel, which I promise I'll write one of these days. It's a good one.) I buried myself in whatever compilations of mountain folklore I could find, looking for inspiration.

Who was this woman, and how had she come to be? How had she lost her leg, anyway? Why was she wandering? From there the stories took shape, informed as much by history as by mythology.

I chose to set the Anna O'Brien stories at the turn of the 20th century, a time of massive disruption in the rural communities of the Southern Appalachians. The depredations of the Civil War had badly wrecked the social fabric of mountain life, leading to escalating spirals of feuding in parts of the region. Editorials argued for the essentially primitive and backward nature of the mountain whites, much as they had done prior to the illegal removal of the Cherokee and other Indians from their traditional lands. In both cases the reasoning was the same: to provide a pretext for taking land. While popular history tends to recall coal mining as the great extractive industry of Appalachia, the logging industry was there first, and offered a stark prelude for what was to come. Industrial companies from the north moved in quickly, scrambling for land holdings; because many mountain farmers didn't own their own land, the companies ran them off or put them to the lease. The ecologically rich forests which mountaineers relied on for sustenance vanished with horrific speed. Most of those who cut the trees down were mountaineers themselves, trying to make ends meet in a wage system that was burying them. By 1900--the year "Wampus Mask" is set--only the deep mountains of Eastern Tennessee and Westermost North Carolina retained some semblance of their original forest. In subsequent years, much of that would be lost, too.

As with the rest of the country, racism and sexism was endemic in 1900s Appalachia, and queer people invisible at best. But while these systemic injustices were widespread, it's a mistake to assume that everybody happily participated in them. There have always been radicals in the mountains, and Anna O'Brien is, in her own quiet way, one of them. I think there's an important place in fiction for lead characters with distinctly unmodern views, people who were on the wrong side of history. In this case, I've chosen to write someone who is, by and large, on the right side. There are usually more such people around then we think.

A word about the Cherokee Nation. Originally naming themselves the Aniyunwiya (or "principle people,") the Cherokee quickly adopted practices of the white governments around them in a bid to stave off encroachment. It did not save them; the Trail of Tears left less than a thousand men, women and children in the mountains of their traditional homeland. After the Civil War, the federal government formally recognized the Eastern Band of the Cherokee and the North Carolina granted them a corporate charter, allowing them to buy back land within the Qualla Boundary. (Anna visits them briefly in the short story "Ghost Days".)

While the amount of the American population claiming "Indian blood" is ludicrously high, there is a long history of intermarriage between the Scots-Irish and the Cherokee peoples. Anna O'Brien is a product of that lineage. By the racial standards of the Federal Government at the time these stories are set, Anna would be considered Indian (if anyone could get her on the rolls.) The Cherokee Nation, so far as we have seen, has not accepted her; therefore she is not, properly speaking, Cherokee. Like many who have partially assimilated backgrounds, Anna's relationship with her status is necessarily ambiguous.

Folklore and folk-music are one of the few elements of Appalachian culture that has achieved some recognition outside of the mountains, in part due to the nation's inexhaustible interest in the "authentic" life of the "primitive" mountaineer. (I count myself here, of course: my initial interest in the subject had to come from somewhere.) Around the time Ghost Days is set, ethnographic surveyors began showing up in hillside hollows with notebooks and meaningful expressions. The folklore they collected was a patchwork left by many peoples over multiple waves of settlement: Cherokee and other indian nations, Scots-Irish colonizers, Eastern European refugees and free black "Affrilachians."

One of the best places to see that is in beliefs about witchcraft. The peoples of the mountains tended to view witches with ambivalence at best and deep suspicion at worst. In Scots-Irish and Affrilachian traditions, a witch was anyone who'd turned away from God to actively serve the Devil, who gave them power in return for their soul. Cruel witches could cause trouble by cursing household items, drying wells and livestock. Some crept into homes to suck breath from sleeping people, transformed them into horses and rode them. Still others cast off their skin and transformed.

Those accused were often marginal people in the community, usually older men and women who had little family support and lived by themselves. At best, they were shunned; sometimes those suspected of witchcraft were beaten badly or killed. The hags of "Night on the Bald" derive from stories told by both Scots-Irish and Affrilachian communities— the skin changing is a property of both, while Hollow Jenny is strongly influenced by the Boo-Hag of Gullah folklore.

Yet there was also a strong tradition in the mountains of folk-healing, herb medicine, midwifery, and in the settling of ghosts. Much of the traditional plant knowledge came from Cherokee practices, as they'd had the longest to work out what worked and what didn't. Similar ideas about beating haints—salt and silver, among other things—tended to pop up in both black and white folk practices. Practitioners of these were sometimes called "witch doctors," or "granny witches," or "conjure women." Some had the second sight, or the water-sense, or other gifts from God. This, too, was a sort of witchcraft, and was often regarded with a sort of wary acceptance. Thanks to a certain amount of cultural reclamation, such practices are more warmly regarded today. These are the source for much of Anna's toolkit, as well as the material in "Hollow Knowledge".

Many of the monsters and spirits haunting this book are my interpretations of Cherokee traditions, and while I've massaged them a bit for each story, I've done my best to keep their essence intact. The Ewah as it appears in Wampus Mask is quite a bit chattier than it is in the original legend, from which I've heavily borrowed. The Raven Mocker of "Night on the Bald" is probably the most famous of the Cherokee traditional monsters in the book, and I chose to imbue its appearance here with both a Lovecraftian menace and subtly pathetic cast. The titular spirit of "Speaking with Tsul'Kalu" is a powerful patron of the hunt in the Cherokee cosmology, and his appearances in traditional tales have him as both benevolent and quick to take offense. Others come from more eclectic sources. The nameless nasty guarding the Herriman grave in "The Revenant Score" is based on the plat-eye, a grotesque shape-shifting ghost of Affrilachian extraction. I tipped my hat to Manly Wade Wellman's hungry cabins in "Where Woods Have Never Known the Axe", and created the

Hog of the Bogs out of whole cloth, though with the full intention that he wouldn't seem too out of place. And in a nod to the folklore the Scots-Irish brought with them, the black dog appears twice, in a slightly ambiguous role both times. (Whether or not he is a good boy is very much up to the reader, but as someone with a black dog of his own, I've got a fondness for him.)

One final note. The mountains of *Ghost Days* are an imaginary place, shaded and informed by fact but not bound to it. The world I present here is one where many of the beliefs of Appalachia's people are as materially real as the historical forces and troubles that weighed on them. This is a tightrope to walk, and I've tried to walk it carefully, to treat traditions respectfully while adapting them to my own narrative. Any mistakes or misrepresentations are my own, and no disrespect is meant toward those resilient souls, who have worked so hard to maintain what the rest of the nation wished to rip away from them.

Anna O'Brien would not exist in her current form--or indeed, at all--without the advice and enthusiasm of Emily Gardner, Maddie Cloud, Marina Roberts, Evan Alvarez, Esa Sofian, Elizabeth Heyne, Olivia Mann, and Ali Whitaker, all of whom devoured drafts as quickly as I could churn them out and politely demanded that I keep writing. Enjoy the book, guys.

This book could not exist as a physical item without the incredible generosity and enthusiasm of our patrons on Kickstarter. I would like to thank, in no particular order: Sue Mead, Sara Ness, Sara Ciskie, Claire Napier, Terry Robinson, K Stellar Dutcher, Daniel Killen, Paul Ringkamp, Mallory Flowers, Julius Csotonyi, Abhilash Sarhadi, Kelda Sproston, Chris Mclaren, Mark and Michelle Potter, Sue Epstein, Jonathan McNamara, Yancey Drake, Kathleen Smith, Valerie Verduce, Eldad Neumeier, Terry Cox, Christopher Hughston, Joseph Noll, Eric Schmidt, Fatima Iqbal, James Trujillo, Ashley Ross, Will McGlaughlin, Adam Rosenlund, Brandon Franks, Joshua Buergel, John Wedoff, Kim Taylor Cloud, Shelby McKenna, Thomas Horstmann, Rachel LeComte, Lissa Treiman, Helen Elbein, K Gourdin, Jason Rak, Devin Adler and Richard Elbein, as well as the many others who donated, spread the word, and offered their best wishes during an immensely trying time.

Special thanks to my brother, Saul Elbein for his role as reader and critic, and for his willingness to indulge in hours of discussion about the finer points of plotting a folktale. Thanks of course to my parents Rivka and Bradley Elbein for their unflagging support and interest. Without them, none of this would be possible. (Not least of which because I wouldn't exist, thereby making writing somewhat difficult.)

I have been blessed with a fabulous team of creative partners; Emily Horne, who delivered such a wonderful design; Gretchen Felker-Martin, who put in hard work making this text as clean and coherent as possible; and Tiffany Turrill, whose humor, passion and eagerness—not to mention stunningly deft and evocative artwork— made collaborating with her a dream come true. I can only hope we'll have the chance to work together again.

GHOST DAYS

SKETCHBOOK

ASHER

The original Anna design owed a lot more to fantasy concept design than it did to any historical costuming. The aspects of her design that stuck were the trousers, coat (initially imagined as more of a jacket) and the big hat. The tattoos disappeared somewhere in the design process.

TIFFANY

These are early ideation and research sketches. After developing a feeling for Anna's temperament, I began the process of "casting" a face, and spent a day doing studies of the features of folks with mixed Native and Anglo heritage, such as these roughs of actress and activist Q'orianka Waira Qoiana Kilcher, who is of Quechua-Huachipaeri / German descent.

Posing roughs! I wanted Anna to be in motion, determined but cautious.

TIFFANYTURRILL.COM

BOG HOG

ASHER

The Hog of the Bogs is an original creation, and I wanted it to be a disturbing mixture of a wolf and a pig. This design owes a lot to an extinct group of pig-like animals called entelodonts, particularly in the proportions and the knobby bits of bone on the skull. (Tiffany's final design skews in a more overtly piggish direction.)

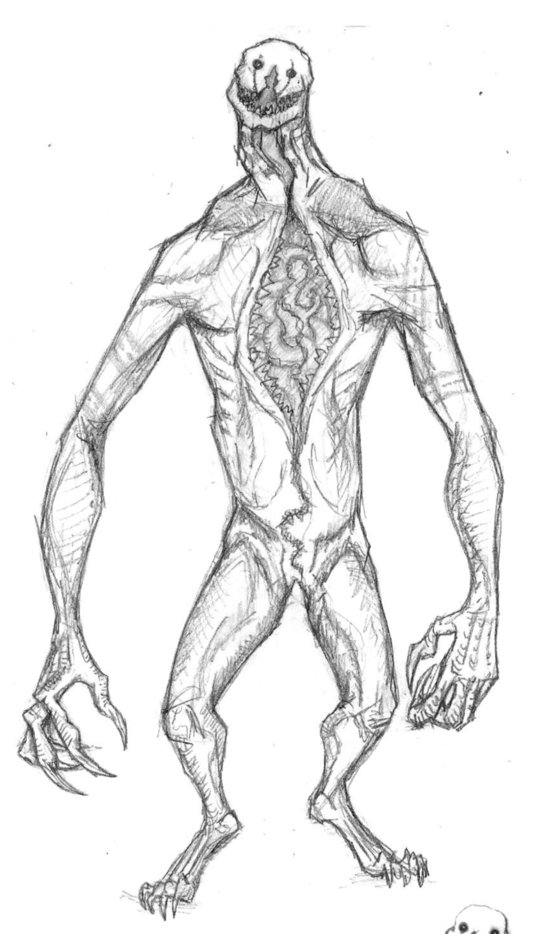

EWAH

ASHER

I originally imagined the Ewah as a sort of horribly elongated humanoid form, brimming with cheerful malice. The original concept was more stylized, with a gaping stomach mouth; a further sketch beefed it up and refined the skull shape. While we ultimately didn't go in this direction, I'm still pretty fond of it.

TIFFANY

I initially envisioned the Ewah as a huge malicious sloth, and gradually began introducing more and more disturbing facial features, eventually settling on those of the Whitemargin Stargazer fish. The manic, distended eyeballs of anime characters and hockey mascots also served to really pump up the crazy.

ASHER

Development art done for Night on the Bald, depicting a hag out of her skin. Her proportions here were a bit too normal for my taste--I think Tiffany nailed it with her Hollow Jenny design!

HAGS

TIFFANY

Early tone and character roughs to get a visual idea of the world, and what level of finish the interior spots would eventually take.

TIFFANY

Not every piece is a success right off the bat, and sometimes it's easier to start over entirely when things get weird.

ASHER

I originally conceived of the Raven Mocker as a somewhat amorphous being, with a mask that didn't quite connect to its body and a cloak that split the difference between feathers, fabric, and shadow. In this version, the body is completely covered. I spent a little bit of time working out variations on the mask and ideas for how it might move.

RAVEN MOCKER

ASHER

Tsul'Kalu only briefly appears in the light, but I took a stab at some character designs while working on a rewrite of the story he appears in. I couldn't resist basing his body plan roughly on a gorilla, but there's some orangutan and circus strongman in there as well. Some of these sketches skew a bit more brutish than I intended, but he's supposed to be legitimately threatening.

ASHER

A development illustration done after finishing the first draft of Night on the Bald in 2012. Hollow Jenny's carcass smolders in the background.

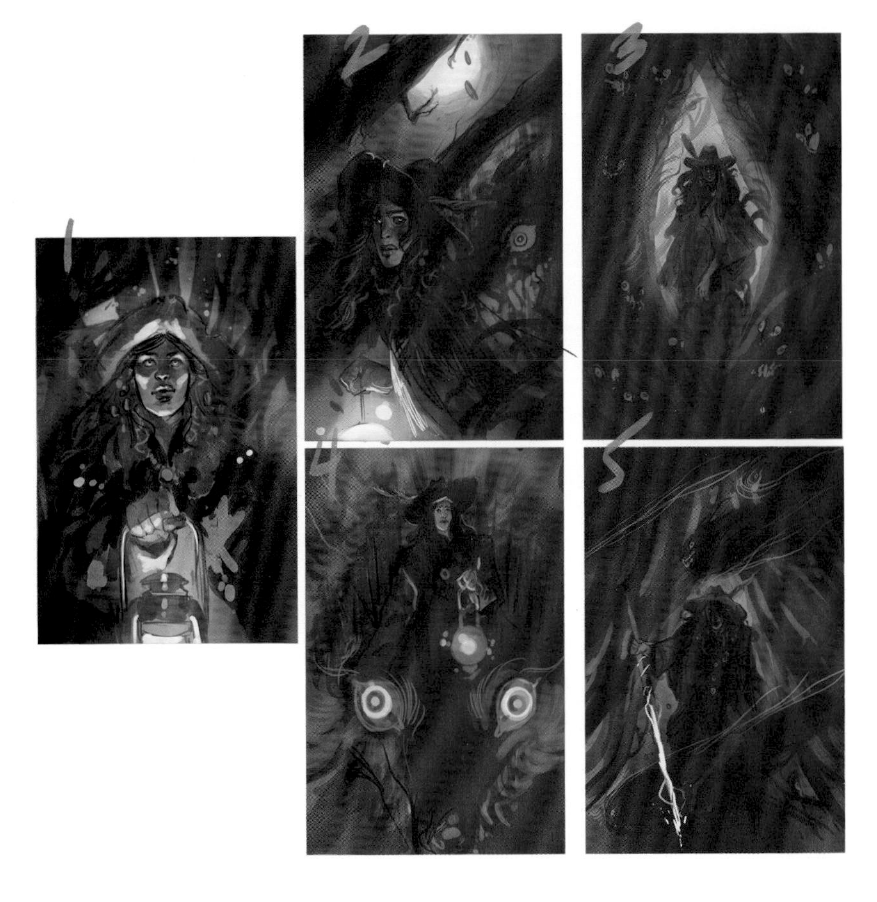

COVER CONCEPTS